NORMA DUNNING

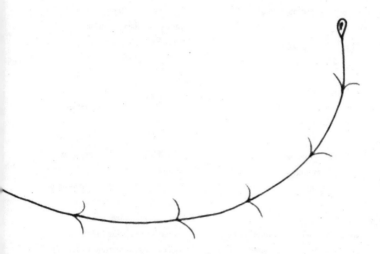

ANNIE MUKTUK
AND OTHER STORIES

THE UNIVERSITY OF ALBERTA PRESS

Published by

The University of Alberta Press
Ring House 2
Edmonton, Alberta, Canada   T6G 2E1
www.uap.ualberta.ca

Copyright © 2017 Norma Dunning

LIBRARY AND ARCHIVES CANADA
CATALOGUING IN PUBLICATION

Dunning, Norma, author
    Annie Muktuk and other stories /
Norma Dunning.

(Robert Kroetsch series)
Issued in print and electronic formats.
ISBN 978-1-77212-297-8 (softcover).—
ISBN 978-1-77212-345-6 (PDF). —
ISBN 978-1-77212-343-2 (EPUB). —
ISBN 978-1-77212-344-9 (Kindle)

    I. Title. II. Series: Robert Kroetsch
series

PS8607.U5539A86 2017   C813'.6
C2017-902061-7
C2017-902062-5

First edition, first printing, 2017.
First printed and bound in Canada by
Houghton Boston Printers, Saskatoon,
Saskatchewan.
Copyediting by Kimmy Beach.
Proofreading by
Maya Fowler-Sutherland.

A volume in the Robert Kroetsch Series.

The University of Alberta Press is
committed to protecting our natural
environment. As part of our efforts,
this book is printed on Enviro Paper: it
contains 100% post-consumer recycled
fibres and is acid- and chlorine-free.

The University of Alberta Press
gratefully acknowledges the support
received for its publishing program
from the Government of Canada, the
Canada Council for the Arts, and the
Government of Alberta through the
Alberta Media Fund.

Canada

 Canada Council   Conseil des Arts
for the Arts   du Canada

 Alberta
Government

This book is dedicated to my ancestors, past, present and future.
These are your words written from my heart. I love you.

contents

1   Kabloona Red

7   Elipsee

35   The Road Show Eskimo

55   Kakoot

77   Annie Muktuk

85   Manisatuq

93   Qunutuittuq

99   Itsigivaa

101   Iniqtuiguti

105   Inurqituq

109   Tutsiapaa

113   Nakuusiaq

117   Qaninngilivuq

121   Samagiik

125   Husky

151   My Sisters and I

199   *Acknowledgements*

201   *Glossary*

KaBLOOna ReD

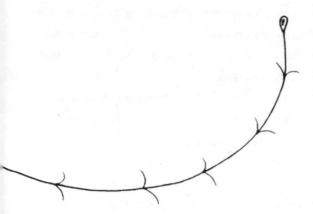

KA-B-LOONA-READ. Kalona Red. Kelowna Red—that's it!
Better stop drinking the wine before noon. It's so wonderful
to feel that beautiful red liquid glide down my throat. It's
like going home, all warm and wonderful. Is there really
anything better than sitting at home, tanked in your very
own kitchen? Husband is off up North, doing his bit for God,
the Queen, and his country. The Queen—remember when she
flew into Churchill? What a day—what excitement there was.
We all curled up our hair, shaved our legs, donned our big
parkas, and headed off to the airport. Excited to see royalty
step off a small plane and wave at us all. Who cared that she
stuck around for only a half an hour—she showed up didn't
she? What a party we had at the Legion that night—all that
old-time fiddle music, all the Elders and the young people.
We danced the northern lights away. It was glorious. Just a
bunch of starry-eyed Eskimos.

Eskimo, now that's a word. White word. White word for white people to wrap around their pink tongues. Esquimaux. Spell it any way you want and it still comes out the same, skid row and all. I should light up another cig here. A rollie, make your own. Always make your own. The North teaches you that. Make your everything. Food, clothes, fun—much fun. Inhale. Exhale. Drag on that homemade-no-filter cig. Get the tobacco stuck between your teeth and absolutely never floss. "Ha," I mutter to the empty kitchen. Ah, the North.

I met him there. A tall strapping country boy from the south. I loved him from the minute we looked at each other. Me, a little Inuk and him the farm boy fresh from the war. He looked magnificent in his blue uniform. I would have done anything for him and I did. We drank and danced and laughed. I felt important. I felt white. Look at me, look at me with this white guy. He gave my world meaning.

We married and I got a new name. I could throw out my old name and no one would ever have to know. They would never have to know about my sisters or my mothers or my father. I could start fresh and new. I could invent a new me. I couldn't get rid of that skin colour though. That was a drawback. Always long sleeves and pants. Wear a dress with dark nylons, sleep in rollers every night of your life and run red lipstick around your mouth first thing every morning, noon and night. People could assume what they wanted. I didn't have to give any details. I would be only his wife. That's all they ever had to know.

We got married 'cause I was pregnant. Oh let's have some more of that Kel Red—let that gallon jug glug-glug into my glass. Bring it to my lips, let it slide down the old pipes. Ah, that's good. Yeah, there was one thing that I was good at— learned it at school too. Young girls surrounded by all those

priests and brothers and nuns. Father Mercredi was the
first. Puts me in the punishment room and leaves me there,
alone, like solitary. Shows up after dinner dishes have been
scraped, spit on and polished. Kitchen crew is gone and there
we are. He tells me to not scream, puts his sweaty palm over
my mouth. Yanks down the heavy underwear—the woollen
armour of the little girls.

Pushes my back up against a wall and rips into my body
like a serpent. I close my eyes and tears drool down my face,
snot drips from my nose. My heart pounds hard against that
cold cement wall. He wiggles this way and that like a snow-
shoe hare stuck in a snare. The pain splits beads of panic off
my forehead. He's finished. Tucks his thing back under his
black robe, slowly peels his hand off my mouth. Mutters to me
in French to "ferme ta gueule—shush, don't talk about this."
And he's gone. I hear his footsteps down the hallway. I slide
down to the cement floor and sob softly. I hurt. I bleed. I don't
know who to tell.

Sister Mary comes in to release me from the room. She
sees the blood dripping down to my white socks. She puts
her hand around my mouth too and quickly walks me to the
bathroom. I try between whimpers to tell her it was Father
Mercredi. She tells me to be quiet. To stay still. She leaves and
comes back with a white cotton pad. She tells me that I will
have this happen to me every month. I try to tell her, "NO!"
She gets stern and says, "Oui, ma chère." She hands me the
pad and mimes for me to place it into my bloody underwear
"between da hegs." That memory makes me giggle now. I
might have been nine years old. Every month—my foot.

Time for another quick shot here. The kitchen clock is
reminding me of that place. Time was everything there. Yep,
I had them all. All the Fathers. First Mercredi, then Father

Jeudi, Father Vendredi, Samedi, and Dimanche and let's not forget the rest of the good old boys—Lundi and Mardi. I never really knew their names. I gave them the names of the days of the week. It all depended on what day they showed up. That went on for six years. Every night.

It was like word got around that place and I was sent to that room every day after school. Eventually I did have to start using that bale of cotton between my legs every month but that didn't stop them. Nah, those old Pères, they weren't about to fuss over something like that. But I learned one thing. I learned to pretend to like it. They learned that they didn't have to put their hand around my mouth anymore. I would breathe hard like a throat song, I would wiggle and I would moan softly into their ears. While they were pumping I was praying. Praying for them to burn. Praying for them to die. Praying to get myself the hell out of hell.

I figured out another thing too. Oh, let's just light a cig. I learned to get good grades. Not just any kind of good grades. I learned that if I became the smartest person in the province for French class I could get moved ahead in my school. I could be like a prisoner released on good behaviour. Marks mattered and I got them. I finished high school a month before my sixteenth birthday. I led the province in French marks. I had become en-française-ized. They made a spectacle of me. They couldn't hide me anymore. They couldn't keep me in the punishment room now. The Bishop even knew about me and came to school one day to shake my hand. While he was congratulating me on this big accomplishment, I prayed for him to burn like the others. I smiled my you-go-to-hell smile and then I winked at him. I was set free.

Oh, the jug is getting empty. Shit, I shoulda bought more of this stuff. I only get to do this when he isn't around.

Otherwise I have to be the white wife. The white wife with the white picket fence, white washed and white dried. Ah, Eskimo—what a nice white word.

Too young to be legally on my own I was fostered out to a French family. I had been in that place so long that I couldn't remember my mothers' faces. My sisters had been taken away from me years before. I had no idea where anyone was anymore. It didn't matter. Most days it didn't matter. I got to be in a real home, in a real house with a real older couple who took care of me like I was some sort of Inuit princess. I had my own room with my own books and a dresser with a nice round mirror. I loved it.

I worked at their restaurant and I started to learn that life was not all bad. I learned to cook good and then I met him. He courted me like I mattered. Wouldn't kiss me on the first date. I changed that. We had a pile of kids. Lots of them. Wall to wall. We moved further north. Camped. Hunted. Fished. Went whaling and berry picking. We took that bundle of brats with us everywhere. Ah, it's a good life now.

You never really get over things. You just move on. Move on to laughter. Move on to being alive. Move on to growing old. And when he's not here, then you can really remember and you can have a sip of Kelowna Red and smoke all the cigs you want. After all, it's the Inuit way.

ELIPSEE

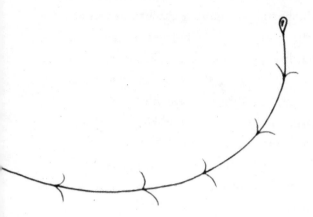

IT STARTED OUT as something we would do once we had put the kids to bed. Pull out the little bag of fluffy green heads, the pretend lettuce, and wrap a nice, white piece of paper around it. Suck it in hard and let it rest in our lungs. We thought we were better than the rest of the people in the community. No Johnny Walker or Captain Morgan in our lives. We were better. White shit booze has rooted its way into the lives of our family and friends. We didn't drink.

We smoke. Tons and tons of weed. We didn't DT ourselves into the bathroom each morning. No puking up rivers of soft brown, no shitting of baby yellow. We smoked only after saying nighty-night to the babies.

Our babies, our beautiful Inuk babies. We made sure there was not one ounce of white in them. We could trace our families back to 1920—better than what most people on the settlement could. With all the proper government documents. We were better than the rest.

Elipsee, she's my wife. Been with her since we were in Federal Government School. Her black hair has gotten a bit of white in it. She still gave me babies, though, in her forties and pushing out little brownies like ju-jubes in a candy store. I've known her always. Hers was the first kiss I ever got. Hers was the first breast I ever touched. Hers was the first crotch I ever cupped into my hands. She is my everything.

She's dying now. I can't imagine waking up and not having her next to me. Breast cancer.

It's got her good and she's coughing out more oxygen than she's taking in. She's still my Elipsee. My homemade girl from our settlement.

The white community health nurse comes in and visits with us. They still think we don't know what's what and how to take care of ourselves. As soon as that blonde bitch leaves, Elipsee looks at me and says the same thing, "Go get the angakkug. She knows what to do."

I have. Over and over and over again. Nothing has worked. We'd stopped eating caribou for a month. We stopped sleeping in the same bed. We stopped kissing. We stopped holding hands on full moons. We have to try this one last thing.

We have to go back onto the land for the full summer. I don't know if Elipsee will make it. We aren't taking the babies. It will be just her and I and the spirits who she will ask for healing. The harder her pain becomes the more dope we smoke. It's eased her a little and at least it isn't booze. There is a lingering stench, a reminder of her illness. The scent of cancer.

Today we are packing. Taking bundles of wood, matches, dope, more wood, matches, dope, tin cans of anything, blankets, a tent, dope, a kerosene lamp, shotgun, dope, more blankets. It's endless. We've borrowed the ATV belonging to my ataata. We're modern Eskimos—we drive Hondas out onto those barren lands. If this time away is what heals her then it will all be worth it.

My name is Josephee. Elipsee calls me Jo. When she says my name I make sense to me. When she says my name I know who and what and why I am. I am not happy to go out onto the land. I like our routine at home. The routine of our tan-coloured babies, Jake and Luke—our twins. Our onlys. They are what keep us centred in this community. They define for both of us the word "joy."

Elipsee says to me, "Jo, the angakkug says to go out towards Nueltin Lake. To stay for the month of July at least. We will find healing there."

I can't refuse her. I never can. What Elipsee wants from Jo, Elipsee gets. She should, she was my first everything.

Today we pack. Pack and pack. The boys run in circles around the Honda. They don't understand that they aren't coming. Three-year-olds don't understand many things and we have never slept a night away from each other. Elipsee might not do so well but I'll be strong for her. It's June 29th. We are heading north, more north than either of us have ever been. This is our one last sure cure. It is our last chance to make Elipsee well.

Papa has left cans of gas in the back of his old sledge. The sledge he used in the pre-Honda hunting days. The days when dogs were your horse-power and got you where you were going. He has even left the runners for the sledge inside, tucked up against a wall.

"Geez, old man," I tell him, "we're only going for the summer." He grins, his pupils sparkle and he shrugs. I laugh and slap his left shoulder. The old man, he's getting skinny these days. No more the broad-shouldered hunter, his spine is starting to wrinkle like his face. He grins one more time, shrugs and scratches at the top of his head.

Taking a breath he says to me, "Boy, there was a time when I would take your mom out onto the land. Those were high times boy. High times."

He winks, shoves his shoulder into mine and laughs. There is something about the thought of your parents fucking that makes a kid shut up. No matter how old I get, I still never want to see that image in my head.

I grin back and tell him to shut his mouth. Tell him I'll say a prayer out there on the land to the spirits for him. He grabs tight to my wrist and gives a whiff sniff as he places his cheek next to my ear. His way of saying "I love you."

Yesterday was the day I brought the ATV and sledge home. Elipsee was so happy. She was going to be healed, the spirits will cleanse her breasts. The gleam from her eyes spreads all the way down to her toenails.

Often I look at her and try to imagine what cancer looks like when it grows inside of you. I wonder what it does when I'm on top of her, pounding away like when we were teenagers. Does cancer get excited, bounce around in breasts? Does it have an orgasm? Who knows? These are the thoughts that take me away from the reality of what our lives have become. These are the thoughts that make me angry for having a disease take over our lives. These are the thoughts that bring me to tears when Elipsee is not in the room. I will do anything for her. I'll even try to get up to Nueltin Lake.

✳ Wind snapping at our eyelids. Blackflies gathering into the crevices of our faces. Travel in the North is never easy. Bouncing, getting bit at and birds circling around us like vultures, only they're not. Elipsee laughs at all of it, grinning and encouraging me.

"Come on, Jo! Let's go! Oldtime!"

Words that spin her into giggles as she lays in the back of the sledge Papa lent us. I've made her a bed of skins. Caribou hides stacked up like pancakes at a Denny's I took her to once in Winnipeg.

We were just a pair of Northern kids out in the big city on a field trip. We didn't know how to order food at a restaurant—hell we had never been in one before. Waitress had yellow hair and green eyes and neither of us had ever seen that before.

"Is she Sedna?" Elipsee had whispered into my ear. We had sat together on one side of the booth.

"There's a name on her shirt—it says 'Edna,' Elipsee." I had whispered back.

The blonde lady gives us menus. We are both thankful for the pictures. Government school had taught us how to read some of the English words but we had never had to try to understand a menu before.

Elipsee is confused and asks what all this stuff really is. We are used to grey porridge and small glasses of milk for breakfast. I was trying to impress her and went into an elaborate explanation of what pancakes are. I explain the flat discs to being something like the bannock that the Northern Crees and Chips make. Elipsee frowns—a definite no. She doesn't want anything that an Indian has ever eaten.

The pale-haired lady stands at our table and asks what we would like to drink.

"Tea!" I said it way too loud but I wanted Elipsee to think I was an experienced city guy, afraid of nothing.

"What kind?" asks Edna who has begun to study her nails, they are bright red. She is chewing something that looks like sap in her mouth.

"Tea!" I say one more time.

The white lady sighs and goes into a long list, ending with a guy named "Earl Grey."

I can't remember everything the lady has said and all I want is for Elipsee to have some tea.

"We would each like some black tea. Is there really any other kind?" I grin up into those sea green eyes and understand why Elipsee thought she was Sedna.

"Freakin' Indians," mutters the waitress. Elipsee and I grin at each other and I squeeze her hand under the table.

"I don't understand why 'Sedna-Edna' has that stuff on her nails," whispers Elipsee. "Why do white women do that? What's it for?"

I was working so hard at trying to be a city guy, I was working so hard at impressing my girl from the settlement. I leaned back, looked at Elipsee and said, "Your anaanatsiaq has the blue beauty lines on her face—right? 'Sedna-Edna' puts it on her hands."

"Oohh," nods Elipsee. "I think it looks stupid." We both giggle, bringing our noses close to each other.

The waitress brings us back little silver teapots with thick white china cups.

"Here. Black tea because there isn't any other kind."

She sounds tired and cranky. I smile and thank her knowing I now have to order our food. I am prepared this time. I am ready. I loudly order two plates of "Moons over my Hammy"—it sounded outdoorsy. Something that would impress Elipsee. We may be in the city but I know it is important to always remember your roots and to honour them.

It's the first time either of us has seen streetlights and roads that are black and smooth. Houses that look nice with giant trees in front of them, and beside them. We think we are in a faraway fairyland filled with palaces. Kings and Queens with gold crowns live in each house. We are foreigners in this cityscape.

"Sedna-Edna" walks past us with a plate stacked with pancakes. Elipsee stares and turns her head to the man getting the plate put down in front of his face.

"Why do white men eat Indian bannock, piled up on each other?" Elipsee looks at me.

"They don't know any better, Elipsee. We can't try to figure everything out. Let's enjoy our time here in this fancy place, alright?"

Elipsee raises her eyebrows—a definite yes. I have impressed her. Taking her into this building called a restaurant. White people cook our food for us. A white waitress is our servant. This is one of our high times.

Two plates are slid under our noses. "Moons over my Hammy" looks like dog barf between two slices of thick bread. Elipsee looks at the plate and her eyes ask a million questions.

As I take my fork into my hand I say with as much gusto as possible, "Aqqaqpuq!" Thinking if we eat it really fast it won't be as bad. We managed every morning to eat the stuff the Government School gave us—this should be easy.

Elipsee explores the food on her plate with her fork. Lifting the bread, sifting through the hash browns, bringing everything to her nose. In the end her plate is not touched. "Sedna-Edna" shakes her head in disgust as she gathers one empty plate and one still full. She slaps a bill onto our table.

As we leave the restaurant I feel angry with Elipsee. She didn't enjoy this field trip detour. My special outing I had set up for us both. I wanted her to see the life of a city person and "Moons over my Hammy" just didn't cut it for her.

"Sorry, Jo." Elipsee whispers into my right ear as we start to walk towards more castles with soft roads. "That food and that 'Sedna-Edna' woman—it was just all wrong. The spirits would be angry with us—we can't do that ever again."

"Elipsee," I moan. "I'm trying to show you a good time here in the big city. Look what you do. You act bad."

We are sixteen years old. We are having our first disagreement. We are in a foreign land and Elipsee won't eat the food because some spirit might get mad at her.

"I wanted you to try something different, somewhere different—the spirits aren't here!"

Elipsee Jonas turns to me with a look in her eye. Her dark pupils glitter like clear night stars.

"Something different, somewhere different? I'll give you "Moons over my Hammy" Josephee Smithers!"

She takes my hand and marches me into the alley of the Denny's Restaurant. In broad daylight she goes down onto her knees and undoes the belt to my grey woollen Government School uniform pants. She looks up into my eyes and she says, "Come on, Jo. Let's go. Oldtime!"

It is the first time those words become our personal mating call.

✳ We've set up our tent. A pop-open and up thing. Blue and brown with a zipper wrapping itself around the oval shape. My momma has given us dried caribou and biscuits for our first supper. We are like two kids playing house on the tundra. Elipsee is happy and we laugh easier than usual. It is as if we have travelled back in time and our spirits have shed the years of work and pain that is normal to any Northern life.

We are the two Government School kids who have been sent home for the summer. We are a pair of lucky ones, we had a bit of a break—others did not.

We went together to gather some rocks and have made our tiny fire pit. A stick with a pot of water is boiling over the embers. We have brought a container of our favourite tea— Red Rose.

"Hey Elipsee, did I ever tell you I met Earl Grey?"

"Hmph, Jo. What did he look like?"

"Elipsee," I giggle as I take out a packet of rolling papers, "He was a big man. Big white guy with yellow hair and green eyes. They say he came to Canada to work at a Denny's restaurant."

Elipsee begins her big smile. The big smile that draws you to her. The smile that makes you fall in love with her and you don't even know why. Her smile is the one that makes people talk with her, telling her their stories without being asked. She is a warm woman. I am proud to be her man.

"Oh, yeah—Earl Grey. He was a king from another country, came here and started a restaurant empire. Right, Jo?" Laughter shakes her belly.

"That's him, Elipsee. That's him. Did you ever meet him?" I'm crumpling green, dried hemp heads onto the paper. I am good at this. A skill I never thought I would have to acquire.

As I take a quick lick at the glue, Elipsee tells me, "I never met that guy but I ran into his wife Edna once." I choke from the harsh smoke and the joke. I hand off the joint to Elipsee.

"Yeah, what was she like?"

"Oh now, she was this big-boned blonde bitch. Liked to brush up her nails with house paint. Always the colour red."

Our laughter fades as we smoke and chew on caribou. It's a good chew and gets softer and juicier as you chew along.

The smoke keeps the bugs away and we sit in silence for a few minutes.

When you have a good partner you can sit in silence for long stretches of time. You are after all each other's shadow. No words are required.

"Jo," Elipsee whispers. I move over and take her hand.

"Jo, I'm sorry I got sick. Sometimes I wonder why it happened. What I did wrong. Who I hurt."

"Ah, now my settlement girl. Don't talk like this. We are here for a time of healing. You never hurt a soul in your life, we both know it."

"But Jo, maybe I hurt one of the spirits. Maybe I didn't even realize it."

Our bums are touching on this little log we are sitting on. Our hands are wrapped around each other. I put my nose close to hers and remind her, "Elipsee, you didn't hurt anything in your lifetime. Come on now. Let's crawl into that tent and let the tundra hear the slapping of pee-pees being pushed together."

Her small hand reaches up to my cheek. "That's my Jo. Solves everything with sex."

I laugh and help her up. As I take her arm, we rub our noses together and I wonder if maybe it was me who has done something wrong.

✳ "Oma, oma, oma, kaja ja kaja ja." Low and rhythmic. Repeat. "Oma, oma, oma kaja ja kaja ja." Again, it's so soft to my ears. I awake to the twilight that is the Arctic at this time of year. Nothing gets dark, only hints of grey.

I sit up and look around our tiny pop-up tent. Shadows are against the one side. Someone is outside of the tent. I can see their form.

"What the fuck?" I mutter to myself—who would ever show up? We're about thirty kilos from home. Not far but too far to yell out for help. I pick up my shotgun. Staying on my belly as I wiggle my way out of the zipper. I have no idea what I am going to say. The only fighting words I ever heard were in western movies—not much help up here.

I slink along on my stomach. Taking baby steps with my belly button. Somewhere in the back of my foggy head is a typical soapstone carving. "Inuit hunting Seal" pops into my head. Some Inuit guy with thick, broad bangs drooping over slits for eyes and an angry mouth. I nervously giggle as I think of how that carving would sell in the south. Southerners will buy anything.

I can see their backs—looks like two men. They are sitting on the log by the ring rock fire pit. They are chanting a little louder now, "Kaja ja, kaja ja."

My finger wraps itself around the trigger. A tiny chill from the metal runs up my right hand. Heartbeat picks up, take in long slow breaths. I squint my slanting eyes and line up the site. This gun belonged to my father and it always has given me food. I'm gonna blast these ja ja fuckers to bits. Splatter the tundra with their trespassing arms, legs and guts. I grit my teeth and feel my finger instinctively wrap a centimetre around the tiny letter "c" on the rifle. I close my eyes for half a second longer than normal and as I purposely tense up my right shoulder one of the men turns his head towards me.

"Josephee!" he shouts in gladness. "You are a hard sleeper!"

"Ataatatsiaq?" I am stunned, shocked. I must have smoked way too much last night. I've read where weed can give you these delusions. This must be one of them. This has to be a dream or some sort of far-out relapse—how long does THC sit in your system?

I crawl out of the tent and jump to my feet all in one motion. Grandpa laughs as he walks towards me.

"Put down that gun, boy. Get over here and give your gramps a smooch!" The words he said to me every time he walked into our house. The last words he said to me as he lay dying on his bed in his tiny cabin.

"You remember Elipsee's ataatatsiaq? Ayaranee."

I extend my hand. We grasp wrists and give one hard good shake. I can't put a smile on my face though. This is all too much. Here I am hanging around with our dead grandfathers and they seem to be enjoying themselves.

"Hey, you look like you've seen a ghost!" Ayaranee laughs and my ataatatsiaq joins in. They start to howl. I feel a tiny bud of the giggles coming up my throat. I wrap my arms around them both and together we form a circle of hysterics. Laughing so hard I think my bladder is going to rip open.

"You guys. You scared the shit outta me. What are you doing out here? I mean, well, you're dead and everything."

The grandpas laugh again. They are bent over now, happy tears pouring out of their faces like faucets running full blast from a kitchen tap. They can't stop. Ayaranee starts to dance and my grandpa joins in. I stand there watching and then step in with them. Wondering if the Pentecostals would consider this to be "Dancing with the Spirits."

We dance, we laugh and eventually they begin to sing their "ja ja" song again. I sing with them and as the singing slows, we each, one by one sit down on the little log by the fire. Silence wraps itself around our shoulders as I put some moss and sticks onto the embers.

"Really though, ataatatsiaq, what are you doing here?"

"Inuuhuktuq, we've come to help."

"Help? How? You're dead."

"Our spirits have travelled over this tundra a thousand times since we each left our little cabins. Haven't they, Ayaranee? We've been watching over you and Elipsee for so long now. Helping when we could. We've come now to help again."

"Arloo, we best tell the boy what we need done." Elipsee's grandpa looks serious.

"There's a few things. Josephee—now that's not even your real name, is it?"

"No."

"Tell us your real name."

"You know it, Gramps."

"Say it."

"Adgekart."

"Where is Adgekart?" asked Arloo to Ayaranee.

Ayaranee shrugs, looks towards the morning sky, shrugs again.

"I don't get you guys," I say. "None of this makes any sense. I'm going to go back to bed."

"Adgekart," says my grandpa, "for now, you do only one thing—you stop smoking that white man's green shit. Both of you. You hear me?"

I turn back and nod.

"We'll see you later today," says Grandpa.

✳ I can't get back to sleep. Watch says 4 AM. Tick, tick, tick. The noise of it is deafening out here. Tick, tick, tick. Should I wake her up and tell her what happened? Tick, tick, tick. Will she even believe me? I can't believe it just happened, how can I convince her? Tick, tick, tick. I roll around in our sleeping bag built for two. Uncomfortable, sleeping on the ground was never my thing. She likes it more than I do. This is awful.

I hear her stirring next to me. "Jo," she murmurs in her sleepiness. I wrap my arm under her head.

"Elipsee, guess what, I just sang and danced with our dead grandpas! They, by the way, look terrific, haven't aged a day since we piled all those rocks up on top of their dead bodies. You remember how they each wanted a traditional burial? Well, somehow they managed to crawl out from under all that weight and 'wa-la' here they are hanging out with me by the fire. We sang a ja ja song, had a dance and sat by the fire!"

Fuck, I can't say that out loud. Only can let it pound through my head over and over again. How can you make sense of nonsense? It was all just a dream. Let it ride. I slumber back into a troubled rest.

"Jo! Quit that laughing in your sleep! Jo!"

Elipsee is shaking my shoulder. My eyes flash open to see the best smile in the world.

"What are you dreaming? Tell me. It makes you so happy!"

I smile and stretch hard. Sitting up beside her I only grin and shrug.

"Don't know."

"Dreams are so important Jo. Tell me."

I figure this is my opportunity. It's my chance to tell her what happened earlier this morning but somehow I just can't do it right now, here in this pop-up tent that smells of our morning breath and sweat.

"Come on. I'll make us some tea and we can talk."

Women, they never let go of anything. They always want to "talk." Talk over tea. Talk over breakfast. Talk before sex. Talk after sex. Talk, talk, talk. Elipsee is a social worker on top of it all. You'd think she'd be all talked out at the end of every day. Not her. Never.

When I move outside of the tent I see her placing some twigs into the fire pit. It is a stunning image. She is dressed in a something both our moms used to wear, with red, white and yellow beaded string earrings floating in the soft morning breeze. Her hair is braided into loose twins of one another. Dangling over the smoke of the fireplace, her face is absolutely serene. Water beginning to boil, she is putting the tea bags into the hot water.

I shake my eyes. This isn't real. Maybe nothing outside of this tent is real. Maybe someone put LSD into that pot. Life has become one long, fucking hallucination! My heart throbs and I am terrified of the beauty standing in front of me.

I back up into the tent. It is my only hiding place.

"Jo—come on! We gotta talk. Come back out here!"

I realize that I have nowhere to hide. I take a deep breath, snatch my rifle and jump out of our tent.

"What are you wearing?" I ask Elipsee. I want to know if she knows what she is wearing.

"A Levi's jean jacket," she says with a grin as she points to her shoulders. "A T-shirt that belongs to my dad and blue jeans." She wiggles her hips and points towards me. "And what are you wearing, husband?"

She doesn't see it. She doesn't get it. She thinks she's normal. I look around. No grandpas.

"Remember those coats our moms used to wear? The white ones with all the beads?"

"Attigi?"

"Yeah. Those things. That's what I see you wearing right now."

"You are trippin', husband! Woot! Woot! What a grand idea. Let's smoke some together!"

"No! We can't! Not anymore!"

"What the hell, Jo? We leave town and look what happens to you. Now I know that you've felt the stress of it all. My sickness and everything but still man, really? I'll get it, you just sit down."

"No!" I grab tight to her wrist "We have to stop! Right now! We have to stop all that smoking weed stuff."

"Jo, what's the matter with you?"

I motion for her to sit on the little log. The log where our dead grandpas sat. I pour hot tea into tin cups and blow on the steam. I look at her and still I see the most beautiful, traditional woman. Immaaluk. She's immaculate, she's so very perfect. She makes me think of a statue of Mary at Holy Rosary Catholic Church. I reach out my hand and stroke her cheek.

"No more, Elipsee. No more." I whisper. I smile. "All this weed we've been smoking since the babies came—it stops today. We are here for healing. Not to get high."

"I can't believe this! You! Of all people! Talking about healing like you give one shit! Come on, Jo. Attigi—like you even know what that is—really! What's up, what's really up with you?"

"Elipsee, I've spent my life running away from it. It's time to find it and understand it."

"Understand what? How our moms made inner coats? What the fuck, Jo?"

"Don't swear, Elipsee. It looks ugly on your lips."

"Oh my God!" she moans, pulling on those beautiful braids.

"What is really happening right now? Are you having a Pentecostal setback?"

Elipsee does this. She throws the years I spent in seminary at me when we fight. We've rarely raised our voices in the last three decades together, but when we do...

"No. It's not about a failed religious career. It's about now. About healing. About you following through with what the angakkug told us to do. We won't travel today. We'll stay here."

"We are supposed to get to Nueltin, Jo. But if you want to stay here for another day, then fine. Whatever."

"Go get the weed out of the tent. Please, Elipsee. We're going to burn it right now in the morning fire."

Elipsee returns. She has all ten of our dime bags in her hands. Two fistfuls. She looks at me and asks, "Are you sure?"

I nod. "Elipsee, I have a lot to tell you this morning. Can we talk?"

"Finally," she sighs and sits on the little log. "How do you know we have to do this?"

"Our grandfathers told me to."

"But Jo, you don't know the old ways, the old life. You run away from it all the time. And why do you get to talk to our grandpas? You? Of all people in our community."

"I don't know why. All I know is that they were here this morning and they told me to do this today."

"Here! This morning and you didn't wake me up! You asshole!"

"Elipsee, please don't swear. Gimme that stuff. It's time to get rid of it."

She puts five of the dimes into my hand. I look at her and ask, "Is there something we should say before we make this offering?"

"Yeah, 'rub-a-dub-dub...'"

"Stop it! Elipsee, you've always known more than me. Is there anything we should say?"

She closes her eyes. Her earrings wave happily at me. Her atigi shimmers with beaded fringes as she raises her pot-filled hand over the fire.

"Isuaruti." She whispers, "That means, 'heal us' OK Jo? Say it with me."

I raise my pot-filled hand as well and together we say, "Isuaruti." Together we drop the baggies into the fire. Together we watch them burn, smelling one high after another move heavenward.

I reach out my hands to her and we lock tight to each other's knuckles. We smile because we each know we have done something right. Today we started to seek something new. Today we started to find what is old.

✳ "Well the pot is gone. Porridge is eaten. Now what do we do, Jo?" Elipsee is cranky. She's jealous. I know she thinks I'm making the grandpas story up.

"Let's go get some birds for supper!" I'm excited. When I was a kid my dad and I would go out with our slingshots and chase birds around the tundra. Oh, it was fun and I was so happy out there with him.

Once TV came into the settlement we stopped. Dad would still ask me to go, but there was so much of the real world to see on the television. Why spend your time running around outside? Besides I was in high school and had plans of going to college. Chasing birds around would not help me any in the real world. The world that existed below the 58th parallel.

Elipsee sighs. Looks straight into my eyes and says, "Like you know how? Come on, Jo. You brought a shotgun—we'll have to kill a dozen birds just to be able to get a half a pound of meat to fry up! God! You'll go out there and blast the shit out of them!"

"Don't be a sour sport Elipsee—let's go. I brought two sling-shots. It'll be fun. Come on! And by the way—stop swearing."

In the tent I find the two slingshots. They were bought to get after all the dogs in the community. Once the babies came and started walking I didn't want the local mutts surrounding them. I used them for animal control, now I am using them for food.

"See. Look Elipsee—see them. Let's go have some real fun."

Elipsee reaches down and starts to fold the blanket from the log.

"What are you doing?" I ask her.

"Taking a blanket. Might as well gather some twigs and moss while we're out there."

I'm impressed. That's my Northern girl. She thinks of everything.

We walk along our treeless Northern desert. I feel like I am looking at it for the first time. It is an amazing site of grey boulders, lichen-laden, tiny flowers bouncing around our feet and the air is perfectly crisp. For the first time I feel like I am walking on ground that can only be called one word. Home.

Elipsee is silent. Walking next to me in her stunning traditional garb. Today my heart is happy. I wish hers was too.

✳ Sneaking. Silently slinking on the cool ground. Pebble perched on the rubber band of the slingshot. Elipsee behind me, holding her breath the way we all do when we are at a horror movie. Maybe this is a horror movie to her.

My hand trembles slightly as I pull the elastic to a taut line. Zap! I hit the grouse in the head. She spins, dizzy from the pain. I reload with another pebble. Zap! Two stones for one bird. This is the best game ever!

She drops. Elipsee claps. I sigh. I can't believe I managed to do this. Geez, I'm good. Maybe I do have a bit of hunter-man somewhere in my DNA. I stand up proud.

"Dinner for two!" I exclaim.

Neither of us say it but we are both amazed by this success. Elipsee smiles that winner smile. She may be getting over herself.

"Jo, congratulations! A good kill! Dinner for two over an open fire—no restaurant in New York would ever make something as good as this is going to taste."

"Ah, now Elipsee. Let's not exaggerate. Those cooks in New York won't know what to do with this—whities."

We both chuckle.

"Hey, see that big rock over there—let's roll it!"

"Rock and roll—old-style, husband?" Elipsee grins.

We begin our game of tundra bowling. When we were kids we used to go out and just roll the tundra rock around. We'd make castles and forts and igloos and cairns. We didn't make inukshuks though. That was serious stuff for serious hunters.

We are sweating and laughing. Rolling, rumbling over the land. Our happy squeals of laughter are the only sounds to be heard. We have it all right now, in this moment. We are all those words that describe happiness. Contentment. Bliss.

Rocks tumble down small hills and we laugh at them. We decide to build a fort and in it all we talk about is how much Jake and Luke would love this. As we build and build and build, piling heavy tundra rock one on top of the next, we ask each other why we have never done this with our own kids.

We have made a jumbled mess of merry rock statues. We stand back and admire it all. I wrap my arm around Elipsee's shoulder and smile into her dancing eyes.

"We need to give it a name." I declare, "What should it be? You, my Elipsee, will name this creation."

I wait as Elipsee's face wanders off to the horizon.

"Saimu," says Elipsee with her eyes grinning into mine.

"Aw, now—Elipsee, now you're getting Catholic on me," I tease.

"How come you know that word, Jo?"

"I don't know. When we are here alone it's like all the words I heard as a kid come back. I don't know why I can understand out here but not in town. I don't know."

"This is good, Jo. Our Saimu—it will greet those who come after us to this place. It will give them the peace it has given us. Let's go back to camp and rest. It's been a good morning."

As we walk back with our dead bird dangling from my belt, we hold hands. In unison we stop and pick up some moss and twigs. We hear only the sounds of the birds around us. We see only the shrubs and tiny flowers and the clearest blue of skies. We smell the cool summer air and think we are millionaires.

It is the first time since Elipsee's diagnosis that we didn't start our day talking about her disease. It is the first time in so many months that we only got up and looked at today. It is as if we have silently made a pact.

We don't need to have breast cancer be our daily focus. We can live and play and fight and still have a life. Cancer, after all, is only a word.

✳ We are back in bed. It's so fun. Being in bed with Elipsee. Hammering myself into herself. I don't know if it was eating the lard-fried bird or the good air or the rock rolling. I don't know which one of them is the aphrodisiac. All I know is this is the topper to a terrific day.

We fall away from each other exhausted. Rivers of sweat are moving in strong currents on our sleeping bag.

"God, that was good!" says Elipsee in broken breaths. I can only nod. What a workout, better than any elliptical machine at the gym!

"I think that was the best time ever. Don't you, Jo?" Here it comes—the talking. I nod again taking a huge bundle of air back into my lungs.

"Best yet," I agree as I try to snuggle into her back.

"How come, do you think?" Here it comes. Make it stop, I think to myself. The deep analysis of why this was the best time yet.

Elipsee wiggles around to face me. I can't get away from this.

"I think it's the fresh air," I say. That seems to sum things up for me. We don't need to go into more detail.

"I think it's cause we burned the pot. I think this is the spirits' way of blessing us."

"Of course. The spirits would have nothing to do with how I moved my tongue around that hot body of yours or the way I used my hands to..."

"Jo! You know what I mean—we're doing the right thing so we get the right thing given back to us."

"Well, let's never go home—let's just stay put and keep killing birds and rolling rocks and all that other stuff."

"Have I offended your manhood?" asks Elipsee, sliding her tongue around her lips.

"I'll give you manhood!" I nab her and tickle her sticky armpits. Her laughter boils over and we both end up tangled in the sleeping bag. A giant pretzel made of down.

"OK, Jo. Stop! We better settle down."

As we shake the sleeping bag into a fluttering, flat square I hear the sound again.

"Ja-ja, oma, oma, ja-ja."

Soft words that are being whispered with a limp drumbeat. Outside of the tent again.

"Do you hear it Elipsee?" I ask, frozen on my naked knees.

"What, Jo?"

"The ja-jas are back. Please tell me you hear it."

"Where? By the fire again?"

"Come with me this time," I ask as I struggle back into my black sweats and a woollen sweater.

Elipsee is still. "Maybe I'm not allowed. Maybe you should ask first."

I pop my head out of the tent and ask in a low voice, "Can Elipsee come along?"

Twin white-haired heads nod.

"Yes," I whisper back to her. "Put on your attigi."

"Right—the attigi that I can't see. Really Jo, we have to talk..."

"Elipsee, please. It's our Elders. Hurry!"

I sit down first. Next to my grandpa. He smells like his old cabin. A mixture of new furs and fire smoke. It's a good smell, the kind you wish they would bottle and sell. "Old Inuit" instead of "Old Spice."

"Hey boy, give your old grandpa a smooch," he smirks.

I lean over and plant the wettest kiss my lips can contain. Then I add a big long lick, covering his entire cheek.

We break into squished chuckles. Bellies moving up and down together. I reach over and snap his strong hand into mine.

Elipsee squirms out of the tent like a worm. Arms moving forward, pull, butt high in the air, pull.

I look over and jab Grandpa's ribs, "Eh, look at that eh! That's mine!"

We both continue our giggling. Arloo hoots.

Elipsee stands, looking confused. "Jo, there's no one here— what's all this about? You're laughing by yourself out here. You made us burn the pot. The angakkug told me not to bring the white medicine so I know you're not on any sort of relaxing kinda stuff. What are you really doing?"

I bring my right index finger up to my mouth. "Ssshhh," is my only reply. Elipsee stands still. Black flies dance quick circles around her body, in the grey of tonight her attigi shines.

The grandpas and I look into the fire and minutes dribble past. My watch and the "tick, tick, tick" of it ring out like a loud church bell.

Finally I look over at Arloo and Ayaranee and ask, "How long should we leave her like this?"

Arloo smiles, "Not much longer. She was a yappy sort of kid. Always asking questions, never listening hard enough." His smile widens. "I'm enjoying having her be quiet for once."

"Me too," I add with a smile. All of us break into more laughter, cackles flicker around the campfire.

"Jo, come on—where are they? Ataatatsiaq! Arloo!" she's yelling. Her cries get louder, jetting across the tundra. Not a sound is returned.

"Ataatatsiaq! Arlooooooo!" She appears to be working herself into a lather of sorts.

I look towards Arloo and shrug.

Arloo stands and opens his arms. It takes Elipsee a few minutes and then I hear her yelp. The same friendly yelp our huskies speak when they see someone they know. Elipsee is in the arms of her grandpa and tears flood her cheekbones. Tears that get mixed in with snot. Tears turning into happy goo and dripping from our chins. I have not seen her this happy in months.

She snuggles into Arloo like a baby looking for a nipple. Snorts, snuggles and more snorts and snuggles. She is in the arms of someone she loves. Grandpa Ayaranee slaps my knee.

"This is all good, boy."

"Ayaranee," moans Elipsee, shocked back into reality. She wraps an arm around him and squeezes herself onto our log. We look like an upright checkerboard. Red, black, red, black.

"Jo said things but I didn't believe him. I'm sorry you guys. I am truly sorry."

The grandpas nod. We each turn our eyes towards the fire. Moments of silence pass. Elipsee and I are waiting. Waiting for their words. Waiting to hear what they have to say. Waiting for the big moment. The moment of healing.

✳ Arloo clears his throat. "I'm not a magic man, a shaman or the angakkug. I am only a man who lived the life of an Inuk. I didn't go to a white man's school but I know a little about reading and counting. I know how to read the sky. I know how to read the land. I know how to read the birds. I know how to count in white ways. I understand how many pelts equals money in the bank and what that money can get for my family. This is all I know."

Ayaranee clears his throat. "I'm not a magic man, a shaman or angakkug either. I am only a man who lived the life of an Inuk. I didn't go to a white man's school either and learned only to read the sky, land and birds too. I understand money, how it works, what it does and doesn't do. We know that your body is sick, Elipsee. We know that you look to the spirits for help and take white medicine. We came to tell you only one thing."

Anticipation grows in the silence of the moment.

Arloo leans forward a little. Looking into Elipsee's eyes he tells her, "Stop the struggle. Unataqpaa."

That's it? "Stop the struggle." We sit as still as possible. Hearts waiting for more.

Elipsee nods as if she understands. I don't get it.

Ayaranee takes a breath and speaks in our language. He is talking so fast that I can't keep up. Elipsee is still nodding. She understands everything. I feel like a broken runner on a sled. Tipping to one side, out of control.

"Hey!" I put my hand up, palm out. "Hey, slow down for a second. I don't get all of what is being said."

Elipsee is calm. She reaches over, pats my hand and smiles that incredible smile. "I do."

"Well, that makes everything better, doesn't it?" I'm miffed. As I strap my arms across my chest I say, "I saw them first."

The grandpas laugh. I'm still annoyed.

"Come on, you guys. Stop that. I saw you first. I get first dibs. It's like riding shotgun—sort of."

The grandpas laugh even more. Elipsee is trying not to look at me but she is soon caught up in the laughter. Chuckles snowball to laughter to hoots to woots to tears falling down on the fire and making small singe noises. The singe noises grow and soon they are like the firecrackers we used to set off as kids on Nunavut Day. It's pouring singes and finally I give up and join in.

It feels like a long time of belly shaking has passed and like the slowing down of a boat motor our laughter gears down to a full stop. Boat motors and grandpas have both faded away.

"Stop the struggle," I whisper as I wipe the tears from my eyes.

"It's just us, Jo," Elipsee says as she looks around. "It's just us."

We wrap our arms around each other, my hand rubbing her bum.

"Well, what do we do now?" I ask Elipsee.

"We sleep. In the morning we go home to our boys."

"But the angakkug?"

"It's O K, Jo. The grandpas said."

✳ I have never again slept that soundly. One night out there in the middle of nowhere brought me the deepest and calmest of sleeps. One night when the grandpas laughed and talked and told us to "stop the struggle" brought me back to where I always should have been.

Elipsee passed away three months later. I never re-married but every summer I take our sons out to our playing spot. Every summer I take Jake Arloo Jr. and Luke Ayaranee Jr. to see our first rock pile we called "Saimu."

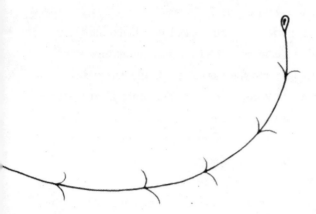

"THIS AMAUTI IS GETTING TIGHTER," she muttered out loud to her empty bedroom.

"I have to wear it though," she thought to herself. Pulling and stretching at the cloth fabric as she bent forward to the floor and then twisting and twisting her back, stretching the amauti over her aging body. Standing up red-faced, she giggled to herself as she smoothed the wrinkles from the greying cotton women's jacket. Maybe white people did this better. They stand upright and zip.

She knew if she didn't wear it then the essence would be lost. One thing white people wanted to see was tradition. Tradition started with how you looked. Her wrinkled, liver-spotted hands, the fingertips bent with arthritis slid along her dresser top. Those earrings with the dangling ulus— where are they? They were important too. She found them nearing the end of the dresser, a little dusty but all she had to do was blow the lint off. Whoosh! and spackled grey dots filled the bedroom. Standing in front of her full-length mirror, squinting her slanted eyes, she felt for the tiny hole on each stretched and saggy earlobe.

She was amazed at old she looked. How had it happened? When did that lady get old? Mirrors were something she avoided. In her mind she was still the bright young lady who had arrived into Montreal with wonderment and curiosity. Her first big city. She had made it to the big time. A real city in those days with the first automobile she had ever ridden in. She had known about cars, seen them when she was in other parts of Quebec. She had just never been inside of one.

"My hair," she moaned—needed more colour didn't it, she thought as she moved in closer to the mirror. Look at those white roots laying on top of her head like a small layer of early spring snow. The time of year the snow fell in thick soggy layers, laying in lines on top of the tundra. Now it sat in the middle of her scalp. In truth, her body had become one big crease. Her face was lined with lines, zipping off in different angles and directions, reminding her that she wasn't a young girl anymore. She sighed and turned from the mirror, thinking again of how round her body had become and how she hated it. Aging was not something to be fought with, but she thought maybe she could manage it better. What if she got really fat and the white people stopped coming out to see her?

Seeing her—how she loved the sense of being on display. Being the focus point, all those round eyes looking at her. No matter what she said they thought it was wise and smart and treated her words like a verse from the psalms. Words that were taken as fact and stored into their heads as a way to understand Inuit. Words filled with awe and wisdom. This act of being on display was something she had polished. She could shine and shine when asked about, "the old life." In truth, her "old life" was not very traditional at all, but the white audiences didn't know that. One thing about white audiences is no matter how much time had gone past, no matter what decade the earth was in, they had a fascination for Eskimos and she played up on their fascination.

If there was one thing she understood, it was how to put on a show. Always be sure to display the coy, shy smile. Answer questions in simple English. Never use words more than five letters long. Keep your sentences very short. Always appear to not completely understand the question and veer the audience off in a different direction when forced to answer anything difficult. It was like snaring a rabbit, something she did with her grandmother as a little girl.

Place the round wire on the path of the rabbit. White person follows rabbit path—they would never make their own way. Be sure the wire is at the right height. White person steps in. BAM! Got him, be sure the wire pulls hard on his ankle and leaves him swaying in one place. There. Got him. Done. Repeat the question asked by white man. Say something funny. White man is trapped in the auditorium. Bead of sweat on his upper lip. Glistening. Look in the opposite direction. Smile. Applause begins like a smattering of rocks on the ground. The sound of applause grows. The sound of applause—nothing made her feel more alive. The sound of applause, the clapping of white hands giving her their approval. It was better than food, better than water. It was better than breathing. She had been born to perform and she did. All of her life was about being on a stage and watching those white mouths saying, "ooo" and "aaahhh." She loved being the Road Show Eskimo. There was nothing better.

Lipstick, the orange coloured one—where is it? Again her crooked fingers searching the dresser top. Why she had never gotten a shorter tallboy she didn't know. Standing on her tiny toes she reached as high as she could to find the black tube. This orange lipstick was the colour that made her brown, wrinkled skin stand out. Important to put on orange lipstick. She had learned she could get away with tracing her mouth outside of the lines. It made her look vulnerable. White women would look at her with sympathy. Lipstick cemented to the outside of the lines, like a picture in a colouring book, made people think you had made a mistake. She knew they thought she was too old to see her lips anymore but if she just went out of the edges by a teeny-weeny bit, the crowd would have pity on her.

"That poor old Eskimo, look at how she can't get her lipstick on properly, poor thing," she could hear them whispering to each other. Sympathy was an important part of every show.

She had been doing this for years and years. Standing on a stage with her amauti that had aged and wrinkled along with her. She stopped dyeing her hair black once she turned seventy. Now it was a soft brown. A colour that was nowhere in her family history. All black heads and black eyes. Oh the eyes, of course she had to put on some eyeliner. Where was her pencil? Bathroom cabinet. All these things she should put into one case but never did. Her road show was scattered all over her apartment.

There, just stand a bit higher up. Damn, twirl the black pencil tip out of the container. Now, the usual question of how long and thick should these lines be? Let's see. The orange lipstick is crooked to the right side, so I'll put crooked lines to the left side of my eyelids. Scratching the pencil over her eyes and just a little to the edge, she grinned, thinking, "My face looks as though it has gone south!" It had. Decades ago. This was a face that had not had the northern winds rub against it for more than six decades. White people forgot that part. Their lack of memory is what kept her road show going.

Looking into the mirror she knew she would be all right today. It was only university students that she would talk to. She could say anything to a student and they would think she was brilliant. Once she had said, "If you go teach in the North, you'll never want to leave." Inside herself she had chuckled and chuckled. This crowd was too young to know she had left as a teenager and never looked back. Only went back once. Never thought to do it again. Period. Because he had come into her life with those blue, blue eyes and had taught her how to do this.

She would often find herself thinking that she had loved him once. This blue-eyed smart man. This white man who had come north to research marine life. She had laughed at him when he came into her community. She could speak English and translate to the others in her group. He had said he was there to study mollusks. Siutiruq in her language— snails. No one ate snails! She had told him that if he was looking for wrinkles to visit her anaanatsiaq. He didn't under-stand. She had dug in some mud along the shoreline and held one close to his blue eyes.

"See the wrinkles on their shell—like Grandma's face!" she had exclaimed. He grinned with all those perfect white teeth. She had reached up into his mouth and ran her finger along his front teeth. He was startled but let her finish. "Nice," she had said. From that moment on they were inseparable. She was with him every moment of every day. He stayed in a tent along the bay that summer and soon she had moved in with him. In the fall she moved south with him when she was sixteen years old. Grandma had turned her back to her and so did the rest of her family. Her northern life ended when he had put his penis into her. She knew that. She didn't mind.

Maybe I should put some lines on my face like Grandma had, she thought. Back to the bathroom cabinet—the blue eyeliner. She stood in front of her bedroom full-length mirror again, pointing the blue pencil towards her chin. One straight line down the middle. Pressing hard onto the pencil she drew one line from her skinny lower orange lip to the edge of her jaw. It looked good. I wonder how many people will think this is a tattoo? Grandma had had tattoos all over her face. An Eskimo equivalent of CoverGirl makeup—something to make you look younger. She grinned to herself. Fooling the whites— now that's fun. From a distance they won't know if it's real or not. She glanced over at the clock. Better hurry. Old Blue Eyes would be here to take her to her road show.

They had never married but that didn't stop the babies from coming. She had only taken her children home once to grandmother. She had taught them to say a few of the Inuktitut words children their age would speak. They had said them when they were around grandmother and grandmother was impressed. It was the only time grandmother had touched her again. Putting their noses close to one another. A sign of approval. A sign of trying to find the lost love of family. She had stayed for two nights and returned to Montreal. Blue Eyes was off in jolly old England visiting his family. He would never have taken his brood of black-haired, black-eyed babies and a woman like her. That was OK with her. Most of the time.

Blue Eyes always had other women in his life. Women flocked to him. She liked knowing that other women wanted him. She liked knowing that he was handsome. What she didn't like is that he slept with all of them. Especially the Japanese. She could never figure out why the Japanese women held his attention. Didn't she look Japanese? She had asked him once what the difference was between her and the Japanese woman who called him from an ocean away and late at night. He had said, "Class" and reminded her that she had never had it. Japanese women had poise and read books. She had taken out a library card and started to read from the children's book section. She loved reading about the Bobbsey Twins and the little girl named Anne who lived on an island like she had. Blue Eyes had told her to read bigger books. She never did. Books were supposed to take you away from your real life and these ones did. She had told him the books helped her to understand white people better. Blue Eyes had laughed and nodded. Day school had taught her only the small words and the small pleasures of young children inside of books that sometimes had pictures.

Taking a brush to her thinning hair, she had to decide what to do. The lipstick went right, the black eyeliner left, a simple part down the centre. She did that. Maybe I should wear the beaded barrette, she thought. Back to the dresser, back on her tiny toes, her right hand groping for the small beaded pin. It's got to be here. There it is. Snap it on the right side. She angled her face upwards. All the wrinkles dangled from her left cheek, fluttering like sheets on a breezy clothesline. Don't do that in front of the crowd, she reminded herself. Hurry, hurry, Blue Eyes will be here.

Today she would speak about The Book. He had written it almost forty years ago. Put her name on it. All about her life when she came south. What she thought of life below the sixtieth parallel. He had made her famous. For a short time. Fame is short. She had read and re-read the book over and over again. It wasn't fun to read like *The Bobbsey Twins* was. Blue Eyes would quiz her on it before every road show performance. He would remind her that this book was his best work. His best-seller and she would not get anything wrong.

Together they had made some money on it. She had learned how to be the Road Show Eskimo. She liked that he would come to watch her speak. Sat in the front row and if she got stuck he had invented the signals to get her to the proper answer. Tap to the right cheek—answer in Inuktitut. Tap to the left cheek—glance away, turn back and smile the full smile. Touching the nose, create a coughing fit and ask for a glass of water. Touching the nose meant Blue Eyes was stuck too. He carried a copy of The Book to every road show. Had flipped over page edges with notes on them. If he couldn't find the answer quickly, he would touch his right eye. That meant to shrug as big as she could, and say, "I don't know everything." This statement usually had the audience say "ahh" and she would add that she hadn't gone to high school or university like they had.

Then the book died away and there were no more calls to perform. Good thing those white professors had knocked on her apartment door a couple years ago. She had suffered through lean times. The kids grown. Blue Eyes in his own apartment. Her alone and alone and alone.

Those white professors made some trouble though. Asking for all sorts of things. Pictures of her life before Blue Eyes. Pictures of her life with Blue Eyes. Pictures of her life now. The now was the hard part. They didn't need to know that she didn't live with Blue Eyes. They didn't need to know he had married a Japanese woman and kept a family with her. His legitimate son. The legal boy with the same blue eyes as his dad. She had finally kicked him out of her life after the boy's birth. Afterwards, it became harder to find road show work.

She had complained to a lawyer. The lawyer made sure Blue Eyes paid her something. Blue Eyes had insisted that she make a personal appearance at his apartment door to get her stipend. Once a month she tapped at his apartment door. Once a month his Japanese wife opened the door with a scowl. Once a month she hollered for him in her language, "Kuru!" Once a month he came to the door with a cheque written in swirling ink. He said the same thing every month in his British accent. "This covers the rent for your flat, a load of groceries for one, and enough to put one bit of petrol into your tank." She would smile her small smile. He would nod and close the door.

The white professors were snoopy, but she had been making some of her own money again. She didn't have to give this money to Blue Eyes like she had in the early days of the show. She still went to his red apartment door, to that penthouse suite and collected what was owed to her. She had been working the show solo until one of the white professor women opened her big fat mouth, calling him to confirm information from the original manuscript. He had come scurrying back like a mouse chasing a block of cheese.

She had to perform for him today. He had said he didn't need the money anymore but he didn't want her to mess up in front of the university crowd. His old research grounds. His old university. She liked having him back with her for the road show. Sitting front row centre, looking at her in the spotlight. Sometimes the Japanese wife sat next to him like a stranger. That felt even better—now they both had to look at her. The ring! Don't forget the ring. She had bought a gold band years ago, wearing it only at road show events he attended.

Tippy-toes, fumbling both crippled hands across the dresser top. Where is it? Panic creeping into her lungs.

Nothing but dust slid from the dresser top. What had happened to it? Check the jewellery box. There was an old picture of her and him inside of the box. A day when they slid into one of those corny booths at the mall before the babies came along. A day when they both could laugh together and at once into a camera. She flipped the picture face down. Ugh, that ring!

She ran off to the kitchen. "Maybe it's in my purse," she thought. The side pocket where she kept her keys. Squinting and squinting and seeing nothing. Turning the purse upside down. Candies and Kleenex spilling onto the table. Damn it! She was getting angry. This isn't good. The ring made those white people think they were The Happy Couple. This was important for him. The retired professor with his Inuk wife. It was important to always have a good public image. It was important to her especially if the Japanese woman sat next to him. Maybe Blue Eyes would know where it was. She would call him and ask quickly. Sitting on the old wire back chair she hit the big buttons on the phone he had given her.

One ring, two rings, three rings. Nothing. An answering machine again with his English accent, "We are not about. Please leave a message at the tone." She slammed the receiver back into its cradle. It was his fault. It was his idea that she was to wear the ring in public. She didn't dare let him buy it. She had headed off to Wal-Mart one afternoon and found it in the young girls' department. Lying there, the round gold ring had called her name among all the costume rings and necklaces and bracelets. A costume ring for her Road Show Eskimo performances. It was a cheap ring. It had to be. It was the way he had always treated her. She wore it as proof. Cheap proof of their pretend life together.

The main entrance door. Buzzer buzzing. Sweat on the palms of her hands. Confession time. She would have to tell him right away. "Come in!" she yelled as loud and happy as she could sound into the building intercom and opened the door to her small apartment. She went back to her bedroom. Sitting on the edge of her bed like a little girl about to be reprimanded. Waiting for his footsteps in the hallway. The clink of his silver cane, followed by the soft squish of his special made shoes against the worn hall rug. Clink, squish—getting closer and closer to the apartment door. She jumped from her bed and ran the short distance to the door.

"I can't find it!" she shouted.

"What now?" Blue Eyes growled.

"The ring!" she said, lifting her empty left hand. She kept her eyes to the rug. Don't look at him she thought. She knew the soft shade of pink his cheeks always started out as before the deep red of his anger would hit the ceiling. She had seen him look at her like this a thousand times before.

"Damn you!" Blue Eyes exclaimed. "It's the most important thing for you to wear! There's no time for us to scramble around this dump you call home. Get to the car! We'll sort this out on our way." Clink, squish. Clink, squish. She let him walk slowly ahead of her. Keeping her head down and watching the lines of the rug scroll past her.

"Today is your biggest event yet," he reminded her. "Everyone will be there, including your publisher and those two women. God, how I've hated what they've done to my life."

He often rambled on like this. Her walking behind, his words filling up the elevator for their short ride to the ground floor. Keep your eyes down, she reminded herself. She trailed behind him out of the building and into the waiting taxi. He did not open the door of the car for her. Something he had stopped doing decades ago. She got into the back seat and let out a scream.

The cab driver's head snapped towards the back. "You all right, ladies?"

She looked to her left and there sat the Japanese wife in all her glory. Blue Eyes had made her dress in a traditional Japanese kimono. She had never been this close to his foreign wife before. They glared at one another. The Amauti and The Kimono hating the sight of each other. Blue Eyes glanced back at them and instructed the driver to take them to the auditorium, while a happy grin spread across his lips.

"For today, you can wear this," Blue Eyes instructed her. Without turning his head, he handed his silver wedding band to her over his left shoulder. The Kimono uttered another bad word in her language.

"Don't lose it and give it back as soon as you get off the stage," Blue Eyes instructed. He was always the man of instructions. Even in bed all those decades ago. She wondered if he did the same with The Kimono.

"But today is only students?" she asked.

Sighing, Blue Eyes turned towards her from the front seat. "Today it is all the dignitaries from Ottawa, and from the university and of course there will be students, but today is the biggest day of your life!" His cheeks turning pink, she put her eyes to the floor.

As the car drove through the city, she put the silver ring onto her left hand. She could not stop herself. She lifted her hand into the air and towards The Kimono. Giving The Kimono her best smile, she winked at her and looked out the window. Her shoulders were shaking with laughter. Another bad word came out of The Kimono's mouth. Her shoulders shook harder. Tears spilled from her cheeks. This was the best day of her life.

Blue Eyes opened his front door while instructing the driver to continue around the block twice more. He nodded at her to get out of the car and told The Kimono to look for him inside. The snarl snaking its way across The Kimono's lips. The Amauti smiled at his awkwardness. Now he might know how she felt at the beginning of every road show. The uneasiness. The big lie that it all was and the way white people thought they were real. Today he had made the mistake. He allowed The Kimono to ride with them. She tightened her left hand into a fist, feeling his wedding band slip to her knuckle. The ring was too big but for the next few hours, it was hers. She held her hand close to the passenger window, letting the sun send off a sparkle. She felt warm inside. This was a good day.

All the politically correct smiling had begun. Shaking of hands. White people exclaiming how they didn't know she was so small. Her exclaiming back that she wasn't. This was the opening to every road show this Eskimo did. The staring, the looks of wonder across the white faces as she posed for selfies with students and in front of cameras mounted on tripods. She loved this part. Her own white carpet. The part where all she had to do was stand up and not say one word. The director of the show came along and moved her into a small room.

"We managed to get you some land food!" the director exclaimed.

"Ma'na" she said. The director looked at her with a confused look.

"Oh, I forgot—that means 'thank you' in my language," she said, a coy grin spreading across her lips. Might as well start the show right now, she thought. Might as well start to play the authenticity card. White tongues wag after each show and it was important to make sure they all thought she was real.

"Well, we have some raw caribou for you!" said the director with a hint of pleasured pride in her voice. "Here, have some now. Enjoy!"

"Tuktu," she said.

"What too?" asked the director.

"In my language, this is tuktu," she said. "It's good for you!" she exclaimed, holding the dish out for the director. The director let out a nervous giggle and shook her head back and forth.

"It won't bite!" she exclaimed as she looked towards the director. She picked a piece of the raw, crimson flesh off the white platter. The director watching her intently, waiting to see if she would put it into her mouth. She did her old trick. The one she had learned in day school when the nuns would give her cod liver oil pills at recess. She put the piece of flesh under her tongue and pretended to swallow. Looking at the director, she opened her mouth wide, waiting for the nod of approval. The nod the nuns would give. Instead, the director gasped and fled the room. She bent over laughing, spitting the raw caribou onto the rug. She walked to her place near the back of the stage, still giggling over her tuktu. She told herself to settle down.

She could hear it. All the shuffling of people into their seats as she stood behind the curtains. She could hear the white professors taking turns talking into the mic about the success of the re-publication of the book that was his with her name on it. She heard them introduce Blue Eyes and she peeked around the curtain to watch him struggle to get up. His silver cane thumping on the wooden floor, the sound of medium applause in the room. He stood. Half-turning, he waved to the audience. She thought he looked like a Jack Kennedy photo she had seen at the library. The Kimono seated next to him with a permanent pout drooping from her red lipsticked lips. "She's no Jackie!" she thought and felt a laugh rumbling up from her tiny chest. This really was the best day, it really was.

At last the auditorium dimmed. The one big light snapped up against the black backdrop and her name was said. She hesitated for a second, and then another. One of the white professors waved for her to come and as she walked to the centre of the stage, the professor told the audience that during her work with her, she had learned what a shy and humble person she was. Squinting into the light, she grinned the half-smile and turned towards the audience. She let the professors each hug her, making sure the audience could see her face.

They were wearing perfume. She hated that smell. It would linger on her and when she got home she would have to put her amauti out on the balcony to air out. That heavy scent would crawl into her throat and she would be tasting Calvin Klein's Endless Euphoria well into tomorrow. She felt the mucus worming its way up her throat. Stepping to the mic she looked to Blue Eyes who had his right index finger on his right cheek.

"Ai!" she exclaimed. Blue Eyes tapped his index finger on his right cheek. That meant she needed more Inuktitut words.

"Ai—again!" she said with a giggle. The audience giggled back.

"Ai means 'hello' in my language," she explained. Glancing at Blue Eyes whose head was starting to rotate side to side, while his right index finger slapped against his right cheek. She had to say more Eskimo words to make him stop. She thought hard for a second and said, "Aqagu ubluqhiut hunu-aniaqpa?" (what day is it tomorrow?). The audience looked at her quizzically. Some smiled a reassuring smile. Some nodded their approval. Yes, she was setting down the snare. She was waiting for those white people to walk down the already-made path. She was getting ready. She was sure she heard a woman whisper that her orange lipstick was crooked. Poor Eskimo.

Blue Eyes touched his left cheek. She turned her head towards the professors sitting behind her and looked back at everyone with a full smile.

"I would like to thank these girls," she said, pointing towards the back of the stage. "I would like to thank these girls for bringing the book back." She put her hands together. The audience joined in. The lady professors bowed. The clapping became thunder. The snare was laid, just high enough above the ground. Now just wait for The Question.

"Now, I could read to ya, but I like to think that everyone here has already read the book." Audience laughs. "And I like to think that everyone here bought it too!" Audience laughs harder, claps again. White people like to clap, she thought. Look at them go. She glanced at Blue Eyes, who gave a slight nod of approval.

"So do you have any questions then?" she asked, searching out into the audience. "Can I get the big light turned off? It hurts me." The rustling of someone running up the auditorium stairs. Snap! Hum. Darkness hits the room. Hum again. Soft lights come up.

A young man stood up. Moved his long curls away from his face as the director ran to him with a mic. "I have a question," he said while adjusting his glasses.

"First, I'd like to thank you for writing this book and I'd like to thank the team of professors who worked with you on the re-release of it. I want to know, what is the difference between this book and the original?" The young man wipes his curls from both cheeks again and looks at her with intent and meaning.

She's stuck, doesn't know how to answer and finds Blue Eyes tapping his left cheek. She turns her head and eyes to the left and produces a full smile, her dentures reflecting yellow under the soft light. Blue Eyes is tapping his nose. He's stuck. She blurts out a full cough into the microphone, making the walls rattle while begging for a glass of water. The audience is wanting to help. People are standing up from their seats. She continues to cough as Blue Eyes fumbles to the first pages of the re-released book. She sees him trying to find his glasses. His left hand fumbles inside his suit jacket. She can't keep coughing. The professors are on either side of her. She begins to chuckle as she sees a picture from one of her library books in her mind. The foot guards in front of a big palace and the Queen of England in the middle. She tells the audience, "I feel like the Queen of England!" The audience giggles.

"Here I am coughing and everyone is worried!" Again the audience laughs. She looks at Blue Eyes who is pointing to his right eye while The Kimono sits next to him grinning.

"To answer your question," she says as she shakes off the professor's grip on her hands, "I don't know everything. I never went to university like the people in this room. I guess I can say the difference this time with the book is these two people, these professors who wanted it back out there. They are the difference." The audience claps. Blue Eyes nods approval to her answer.

"You know," she continues, "this book has really been the thing that has bugged me most in my life. I would like to really talk about it."

Blue Eyes shakes his head in an emphatic "NO." She looks at him and grins.

"The book really belongs to him," she said, pointing to Blue Eyes. "He's the reason the book was ever written." The audience thinks she is telling them her husband is a nice, sweet guy. There is a smattering of applause in the crowd. Blue Eyes looks around and gives several polite nods of his head. The Kimono sits up a little taller, a little prouder.

"As a matter of fact, he wrote it!" she yells into the mic so loud that the speakers hanging from the walls vibrate a long electronic sigh. The audience wiggles. The only sound is of air sweeping into their lungs. The Kimono leans forward to stand.

"There! After all these long years! I'm finally saying the truth!" she yells. "He wasn't getting anywhere with his research and he hated teaching all you university kids so he sat down and wrote it! The truth is I can't write a full sentence without making mistakes. He likes to talk about my mistakes," she says. Her eyes feel damp. One of the soft lights is bugging her. The professors come in close to her again. She feels her foot guards on either side of her. She is tired. Tired of this game. Tired of this pretend life with Blue Eyes. Tired of The Kimono who ruined everything in every way.

"I'm an old woman now," she says as she clears her throat, "I want to tell my truth."

The audience squirms. Blue Eyes struggles to stand. She can hear the thump, squish of his cane coming towards her. The foot guards move in closer. One leans into the mic and asks, "What do you mean?"

"I never wrote one word of it! The book is a big lie. He did it!"

Blue Eyes is using all his strength to climb the side stairs of the podium. He is straining. His face is red. His anger is percolating and ready to explode. She sees it and snaps onto the hands of the professors next to her. Her tiny body trembling. She feels her heart tip-tapping inside of her. She's got him. At last. She got him back.

Today is the best day. Today is the day she will tell her truth.

Blue Eyes comes close to the microphone. He can sense the confusion of the audience and he leans down into the mic and says, "Don't mind her. She gets like this. It's her age." He says sympathetically into the mic.

"I believe the medical term is something about 'early onset'," he says smoothly into the mic.

The larger professor moves her head in front of Blue Eyes and tells the audience, "I think we need a break. There are refreshments out in the hall. Why don't we all just take a moment away and reconvene in fifteen." The audience hesitates, and begins to shuffle out of the auditorium, murmuring to one another and glancing back to the stage over their shoulders.

"I have to take her home now," Blue Eyes tells the professors. "She must not have taken her medication today." He moves his arm around her shoulders.

"We can't leave the book launch like this!" exclaims one of professors. Her large glasses bob up and down her nose, "You owe us an explanation! We worked hard to get this book back out there—tell us the truth!"

Thump-squish. She walks along behind Blue Eyes again. Her own eyes looking at the wooden floor. "Come back!" she hears one of the professors yell. She continues on behind Blue Eyes knowing that after today she will never see him again. Knowing she has made the biggest mess out of the best day. The Kimono stands at the bottom of the stairs and smiles. She has won. At last all of this is over and she can have her life with Blue Eyes. The Amauti has made the biggest mistake ever. As she steps off the last stair, she takes the real wedding ring off her left hand and puts it into The Kimono's outstretched palm.

"He's all yours," she says to The Kimono in a defeated whisper.

She returns to her empty apartment. She returns to her empty life. No children. No grandchildren. No great grand-children to greet her. She is completely alone. She feels some sadness, but in truth it feels like a big weight has been lifted from her. In her old age, her spirit is light. Tungasuttuq. She is at ease, pleased.

She sits next to the phone waiting for it to ring. She knows one thing. Those professors will want to know her story.

She looks at the big numbers on the phone Blue Eyes had given her and from memory dials his number. Today had been the best day.

Kakoot

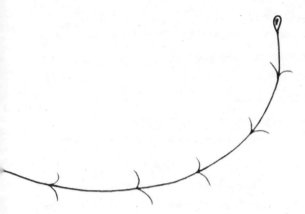

THE FLUORESCENT LIGHTS BUZZED over his head like a swarm of black flies. They were everywhere. Kakoot reached up to swat a clear path out of them when a voice spoke.

"Hey, hey now Mr. Tootoosis, just relax. Lie back down, champ. There you go, just have a little nap." A needle pricked his arm and he faded into a blackness that only medication can give, a blackness that you can't fight your way out of.

It was shuffling day at the nursing home. Shuffling happened at the beginning of every month. The day when you were re-assigned to a new section if your number came up. He lay sprawled on his tiny stretcher, waiting to be taken to the yellow pod. Yellow meant you were on your way out. He was on his way there now and he knew it.

This was a progressive place all right; a place where you were handled like a traffic light. The red pod when you first entered the home, if they considered you functional. Functional meant that you could get yourself to and from the bathroom. Functional meant you recognized your name when it was called. Red was a place where they wanted you to stay for as long as possible.

Green meant that you were becoming dysfunctional. No longer the keeping of piss and shit to yourself. In the green pod, you started to share it with your inner thighs and your kneecaps. This was the first sign they looked for. No turning of your head when your name was called, staring straight forward was the only response. Green was the breaking point.

Green, the place where the rest of you began to fall apart. Piss, shit, spit and sperm, all bodily fluids were released without rhyme and definitely without reason. Your body was a tap of fluids being turned on and sprayed at random. The response from the staff was a hose, beating back your self-made liquids and splatting your skin until it began to peel. Green was the place where you wanted to stay for as long as possible.

Green led to yellow. Yellow was the door with the neon sign over it: Exit. The last door, the last hurrah, the last breath. It was where you were taken to die. Where you were taken to piss and shit your way into the next world.

Lying on that gurney gave Kakoot a chance to remember. Those Kabloona, he thought, they took everything away. My name. My family. Especially my mom. In return I got their white name. Not one but two. Front and back. Everything in its perfect order for their perfect lists. They changed it all but none of that matters now. I am going home.

The Old Ones taught me when I was young to not fear death. Welcome becoming one of the alliit, the Under Ones. In white time it would take over a year to get to The Land of the Dead. I know I have to crawl under that big skin carpet, getting squished until my body is flattened.

Kakoot smiled at the thought of his entrance into the two worlds on the other side. The worlds beneath the oceans and rocks. He would eat his land food again and above his head blueberries would droop, waiting for his fingers. He would become an Under One. He would be beneath the earth but it would not be Hell. Hell, the Old Ones had told him, did not exist underneath the water and land. Hell was this yellow-walled room and he was leaving it.

The spirits gathered rocks into a circle in the rocky bay. They placed the biggest rock in the middle for Sedna. Not a word was spoken among them. Not one whisper was carried on the wind. They could not have her ask, "Taima?" in that icy, slicing voice. The voice that only she had. They couldn't leave Kakoot to wander alone on the tundra. He was preparing to become an Under One and come to them. His name had to live on within two days of his death. Sedna sat in the centre of the spirit circle. "Is anyone in your community expecting a baby?" she asked crisply.

"No," the others responded. She sighed. "Well, are any of their dogs pregnant?"

Kakoot opened his eyes. He was still in the traffic light hell. He didn't like this home, this home of colours and rules and lights that buzzed in your face and eyes and ears. He didn't like the electric black flies that crowded over his nose, digging into his ears, living in his tears. He wanted only to get out of here. Go home. Die on his tundra. Buried under a pile of rocks. Not here. That's what he wanted and he was going to get it.

Sedna, her hair knotted and twisted into lumps of pain, demanded that the other Spirits begin to run their fingers through her hair. They obliged her immediately. The fingers and thumbs combing through her hair was the best way to soothe her. The Spirits knew this. She began to moan. Having no fingers or thumbs made life inconvenient in so many ways.

We have been nothing but an inconvenience to them, Kakoot thought. He had places to be, but his arms and legs were useless. He thought that this must be how aggaituq must feel. A voice drifted into his head. "There now, Mr. Tootoosis, sit up now." He felt a man's grip on his lower back and heard the same female voice. "Good. That's the way a champ is. Right, Mr. Tootoosis? Here you go, in your brand new room. Aren't the soft yellow walls lovely?" As his body slumped onto a high-backed chair, he felt the thick belt wrap cruelly around his wasted waist.

They had no respect for the aged in this place. Here, their word was final, not his. At home the old people understood everything. It was simple. They knew that the knowledge of the ancestors had been passed to the old people through their mother's milk. It stayed in his blood. If he were at home he would be treated with pillurittitaq, like someone who is worthy of great favour from his people. He had obeyed to the spirit voices all of his life.

"We must get Kakoot to the Land of the Dead within forty-eight hours," he heard Sedna say. "One of you go the hospital and find a woman in labour. Make sure her pains are not too fast right now. Put some of your medicine inside of her. The rest of you begin to build the qalgiq. We have someone important to celebrate! Kakoot needs a house to come home to!"

"But Sedna," the Caribou Spirit countered, "he is in a white house now. They call it a nursing home. He will die in his krepik. He must go the Land of the Day and become one of the People of the Day."

Sedna's face brightened to yellow. Her face glowed like the midnight sun. Her lips snarled, "He is one of us. He is an Elder.

He is respected. He knows the old ways! He will come to the Land of the Dead. I have chosen him."

She turned to the Caribou Spirit who had dared to speak. "I have final say here. No questions! All the rest of you go build the qalgiq! I will be sure the hunters have good luck today for our welcome feast." Her eyes stared into those of the frightened Caribou Spirit, "Except you. You have the head of a caribou but that rest of you is all man. You will continue to stroke my hair." A delicious smile ran across her mouth, "and other things."

"There now, Mr. Tootoosis, what a fun name, we'll just let you sit up and look around at your new home."

As the nurse's shoes squeaked their way from his room he looked into the eyes of a black man. A big, black man who leaned in close to his face and said, "Well done Skeemo, now you just stay put. No blabbing in that native tongue today—got it? We heard you're a screamer and we won't have any of that around here. It's quiet, always quiet, 24/7. No muktuk, mukluk, or what the fuck—got it Skeemo boy?" His huge, dark hands dug into Kakoot's shoulders. Kakoot knew purple fingerprints were beginning to form under his purple polkadot hospital gown.

Kakoot could feel his arniniq begin to drain out of him. Warehousing the elderly in nursing homes was cruel. Elders needed to wander away on an ice floe, but the Kabloona knew none of these things. They wanted to keep him strapped to this bed where he could do nothing but drift away in his head.

"We forget," Sedna began as she slid her back into the belly of the Caribou Spirit. "We forget to honour our ancestors' ways. What has happened to all of us spirits? Kakoot is one of the good ones. We can't bring him an ice floe and let him choose his time like we used to be able to do. These are the things that happen when Eskimos go south!"

She saw the sideways teardrop-shaped eyes of the Caribou Spirit nod in approval.

"You answered correctly!" Sedna leaned in a little closer and whispered, "Now, let me see the size of those man hands."

The big black one, the one with big hands, always called him "Skeemo"—like he hadn't heard that over and over and over again. They all gave you names. Names that no one ever got right. Saying your name right meant you were real, that you existed, and there would be none of that in this white house. One white institution after another, that's all his life had added up to. Mission folks who told him God loved him, he already knew that. Mission folks who changed his name from Kakoot to Amos.

The spirits had chanted his name into the ears of his anaanatsiaq. She had heard it in the air and with her heart she had gifted it to him. His grandmother and those from the Land of the Dead had brought the worlds together inside his spirit. His name had given him the strength and skill of those from beyond. He carried his name with careful pride, always mindful of the expectations of his own people.

Kakoot had been given many names by his people over time. It did not cause confusion. But the missionaries had given him a biblical name—to avoid confusion, they said. His mother had let them give him that other name, but she only used it when a mission person was present. Otherwise, she whispered "Kakoot" softly in his ears when waking him or when putting him to bed. Called it to him when he was outside and needed back indoors, sang it to him when she washed down his tiny body and at times yelled it to him when he was in danger. His mother—he had loved that woman more than any other woman in his lifetime.

In the stump that was her hand, Sedna kept turning the Caribou Spirit's fingers this way and that. "You know he was named after his grandfather. His grandfather was a great hunter and Kakoot was given his name, and his spirit at birth. It was a good birth. He lived up to his grandfather's skills. All the spirits had chanted him into the world. I knew then that one day he would be The One." Sedna looked again into the Caribou Spirit's eyes. She lowered her voice to a sultry murmur, "Will you be The One too?"

Qungaluttuq, that smile of embarrassment, spread across Kakoot's face. There are some things that he should not hear from the spirit world but he understood this kind of woman. Women were divine creatures. Sent from the heavens to give you pleasure, warmth, and someone to eat a meal with. Someone to talk your day over with, someone to cuddle up to on those cold snow-filled nights when the wind howled longer and louder than any wolf. Women, they made you happy; they broke your heart. They were the charms of all of your life's bracelets, they were only memories now. He had loved them all his days, he loved their sound, their swoosh, their smell. Women, there had been so many of them.

Sedna could feel the Caribou Spirit's body wiggling away from hers. "I am the Goddess of the Land of the Dead! You can try to get away but you know that I will make the people suffer. Do you dare to risk that? They have lost enough already. Even their names are no longer their own." Sedna wrapped her elbows around Caribou Spirit's ankles and dragged him back into place. "I would advise you to do as directed," she cautioned him.

Kakoot glanced down at his shrivelled penis and gave a short laugh. Now he only ate his oats but never sowed them. He sighed and looked towards the narrow window injected into the soft yellow wall. It was snowing. A good snow. Pukaangajug.

The days of making snow houses with his family had slipped away so quickly. Simple days, days of building, hunting, and fishing. Days of laughter and happiness. Days of having only two concerns, food and warmth.

After the mission came the schools. The white schools that taught him how to write with a pencil and pen. Schools where he became "Amos Tootoosis" and later was given a number: W-4369. For many years he wore his leather tag around his neck. He stopped feeling that it was there. It had become a part of his skin, a part of his heart. W-4369 replaced "Amos Tootoosis." He was called by it in school, on his mail, and for a joke his family had painted it onto the front door of his house. Telling him that he would never go into the wrong house after a night out on the town.

Sedna picked up Kakoot's thoughts from the rocks where they had landed. "Remember the numbers, the tags and not one thing that any of us spirits could do to stop them?" She raised one of the Caribou Spirit's hands onto her wrists, "Get back to straightening my hair! We'll begin again." Sedna lay back in the warm comfort of Caribou Spirit's belly and sighed.

Amos Tootoosis was a tinier, weaker version of the hunter and lover he had once been. Today he was Amos Tootoosis, member of the yellow pod, exit stage left. He sighed again and jerked the tall-backed chair towards the window. Good snow, snow that was hardy and ready to be turned into a house, tea, broth, and a face wash. Good snow.

"Well, look at you Mr. Loose Tooth, you managed to get your-self over to the window. My, you are a strong one!" spoke the squeaky-shoed nurse. They all did this, assumed that he couldn't understand one damn word that fell out of their mouths. They compensated by talking in louder than normal voices as if they were talking to a newborn or a puppy. They all got his name wrong too and he was long past correcting them.

"Faster with the combing," Sedna instructed Caribou Spirit. "We used to sing and drum the babies into the world. Our birthing love songs were the best. Where do you suppose the Spirit who went to the hospital is? You go find out what is happening. And don't dawdle." Sedna smiled that smile that always lies somewhere between evil and good. The one that leaves the receiver unsure. "You never want to leave me waiting. Ever."

Kakoot did not want to make her wait. He could hear the drums of his ancestors calling his voice into singing. He began to chant a drum song from his childhood in his head, one that made people happy. Atuvalluk, a song of love.

To the white world that now contained him, Kakoot smiled. He had learned to years ago when dealing with the whites. Always smile, always nod and as soon as they were gone, go back to who you really are. The white people would say that the northern heathen savages were ever so passive, accommodating, and child-like, but the reality was that not one of them gave a good god damn. Kakoot, Amos Tootoosis, W-4369 had lived through it all but had decided he would never die here, not this way.

Caribou Spirit spat out all his words at once, "The Hospital Spirit has slowed the labour pains of a young woman in the hospital. He is wondering how much longer he has to keep her like this?"

"How long?" Sedna screamed, "How long? What the hell is wrong with you? The new baby arrives in the way of welcome that our ancestors showed us. What I want to know is, is he whispering the name 'Kakoot' in the mother's ears?"

"I don't know." Caribou Spirit's Caribou head looked past her.

"Then get back there and tell him to!" Sedna screeched. "And then, you will return to me. We have a transaction to complete before this day ends." Her arms shaped like boat paddles shooed him away.

Kakoot mimicked the boat paddles that he saw as he tried to wave the nurse away, but she had more to say. "Your lunch will be here shortly, and well, I guess you're okay for now. After nap time we are having a little social in the main fireplace area today—you'll be coming. See you later Mr. Too-Much-Moose— my, what a name!" Then she was gone. The sound of nylon against nylon as her round legs and squeaky shoes left the room.

Kakoot closed his eyes. It was the best way to handle all white places. Close your eyes and remember. Remember the days of the hunt, the days of preparation for it, the days of watching over the land and waiting for the herds to come. The days of patience and planning, the happiest days of his life. He could smell the cold air, he could see the browns, yellows, and soft greens, he could hear the multitudes of birds that arrived each spring. When he closed his eyes he was young again, he was strong, but most importantly, he was free.

"Where are the hunters?" Sedna shrieked. She had to get everything in order. The new baby was coming. They had to name him Kakoot. The Spirit Drummers and Dancers had to be ready to go. The time was fast approaching. The feast had to be in order. Order, these Spirits needed order. Order, that was something the Spirits had lived through. They would understand her.

The sound of a wet, sloppy mop made Kakoot jerk his eyes open. He snapped his head over to one side and saw a janitor in navy blue pants and a matching short-sleeved shirt. He had a nametag with the word "Wade" written on it.

"Hey pal," said the janitor. "You're new. I'd shake your hand but I'm a janitor and touching a patient is considered cross-contamination of the worst kind. Well, what do you think of your new digs?"

This young man spoke in a regular voice, but Kakoot could not hear. He waved to Wade, motioning him to come closer to the window.

"Look at all that fuckin' snow! It's gonna be one big, fat bitch to try and get home tonight. Lucky you, you don't have to worry about driving in this shit."

Wade started back to the door, the mop dancing half number eights all over the floor.

"Aniguititsijuq," said Kakoot.

"What?" Wade turned around and started back into the room. "You old timers, you're always saying shit that doesn't make sense. What can I do?"

Kakoot turned his dark eyes directly at Wade. He spoke softly, slowly. "I need your help young man. I need you to help me get out of here."

"Listen, Mr. ...what's your name here? I'll check the door," Wade walked back to the door, looked at the white tag with the name "Amos Tootoosis" imprinted on it.

"OK, listen Mr. ... Shit, I don't know how to say that name. Listen Mr. Amos, I can't do anything extra for people around here. They'll whip my ass, I'll lose my job, and then what'll happen? We all want outta here."

The Spirit Hunters stood before her. At her feet lay caribou piles. Stacked one on top of the other in groups of five.

"Is this enough?" Sedna asked. Her mouth drew tight to her face. No one could ever please her. Each Spirit Hunter looked away into the empty space of the Land of the Dead.

"We are bringing home Kakoot! We need more meat. He's been off in the city without any of the real food that he grew up on. This is a welcoming party. Go out and get more!" The Spirit Hunters shuffled away.

"My hair!" screamed Sedna. "I will allow the Spirit Hunters' kill to grow only after my hair is untangled!"

Two old four-legged Women Spirits came forward and dug their sixteen fingers and four thumbs into the mass of knots.

They rocked on their eight legs behind her and began to hum the Song of Love.

"Stop it!" scowled Sedna. "I know what you're trying to do."

"You love him," said the oldest of the Old-four-legged Woman Spirits.

Wade looked Kakoot straight in the eyes. "How about I do this for you instead?" Wade leaned over and whispered into Kakoot's ear, "Do you want a cigarette?"

Kakoot chuckled. This white boy was not so bad.

"Yes," Kakoot answered even though he didn't smoke.

"Okay, here's the deal. After lunch they come around and put all you guys into your beds for naptime and then after nap—because today is Friday—they take you to the fireplace area where you each get to drink one glass of draught. It's shit alright. It's the cheapest, ugliest tasting crap that they bring in from The Empress Hotel. So how about this: before they come to get you up from the nap, I'll come back, get you into a chair, and we'll go off to my office for a smoke—alright?"

"He is chanting 'Kakoot' into her ears over and over again," reported the Caribou Spirit. With fear clipped to his voice he added, "I will fly back to him once you give the signal to increase the labour pains. He says that in her sweaty discomfort she is now saying the name 'Kakoot' out loud."

"Good news," snickered Sedna. "Leave!!" she screamed at the old four-legged women. Her arms rotated like a boat propeller as she sent the women off at a jerky run. She looked back at the Caribou Spirit and asked, "How do you have sex with those big antlers on your head?"

Kakoot nodded. His day now had a purpose. He had something to do besides remember. Kakoot looked at Wade letting the crow's feet of his eyes begin to take flight.

"That sounds good. Now, you said you're not allowed to touch people but allow me the honour of just one thing, young man. Allow me a quick handshake. After all, we appear to have a gentleman's agreement." Kakoot put his wrinkled, brown hand forward. Wade's mouth was hanging open in amazement as he put his strong, white hand forward. They shook hands and surprised each other with a small, extra squeeze as the shake ended. They grinned at each other. Each had found a friend.

Lunch had been the usual soft, mushy stuff. Stuff without flavour, stuff without texture. It went into your mouth and you didn't have to chew. Open, swallow, open, swallow, take another breath, open, swallow. Done. All the meals were like that here. There was never choice, there was never smell. It was food that lacked aroma and food that smacked of arrogance. As if you were deemed by age to no longer yearn for the taste of home. He missed his food, his food. His tuktu, his fish, his whale. He missed the feeling of a good chew, the gnawing and grinding of teeth against solid substance.

Even some dried fish would be better than this swill they called food. Fish that he used to catch in the spring and summer to feed to his dogs in the winter. His dog food would taste better than any of crud that arrived on a tray tucked under shiny steel domes. Eat that lunch, get it done and soon they'll tuck me away for a nap.

Kakoot was tired of many things but mainly he was tired of not being able to eat something that mattered.

"Well, Mr. Goose-Goose," said the nurse, returning with the big black man behind her. "We're here to tuck you in for a snooze, how about that!"

Kakoot could feel his body oozing out of every pore. It was starting. His body was freeing his spirit.

Caribou Spirit strutted towards Sedna with confidence, "Well, let's give this sex thing a try and find out," he said. His big caribou nose glistened with taliut. Sedna stepped back and glared at him.

"I'm so glad I never married! All you men, you're all the same! I would rather live like this," she said, waving her fingerless palms in the air. "My father thought he had punished me by cutting off my digits, but look at what I have done with that. I take care of my people and that is my purpose. You—you were just a small afternoon possible delight. Fly back to the hospital. It's time! Send the old women back in!"

Kakoot heard the squeaky nurse coming down the passage. Good God, he thought, this nurse is worse than any teacher I ever had a school. Maybe being called by his disc number hadn't been so bad after all. Ah, she'd get that one wrong too. He looked up with the obligatory smile across his face. Just smile, just smile and know that this whitey and one black guy will leave. He felt the big square black hands scoop him out of his chair and smack him into this bed. He didn't moan, he didn't blink. He'd won bigger battles with bigger people in his lifetime. Just smile and know that will all end shortly.

"You're a nice quiet Skeemo, aren't you, Amos?" said the black guy, his square teeth close to Kakoot's eyes, a chuckle erupting from his dark throat.

Kakoot closed his eyes, waiting for his memories to stop in for a visit. She would come again to see him, his mother. She usually stopped in at this time of day. They would talk about their times together when they were both so much younger and stronger and life had a northern ease to it.

Sleep began to wash over his body and he could hear them. The birds, millions of them, so many kinds, flooding the tundra floor all at once with their gooey shit and yelps louder than any of his dogs. Spring. The best time of year. Time to get ready for the hunt, time to prepare, time to take stock. He could hear the rhythm of his breath and feel the rise and fall of his chest. Sleep was his hinterland, his escape.

"His mother is preparing him, isn't she?" Sedna asked of the Old Four-Legged Women Spirits, whose cooked fingers were growing increasingly numb.

"Aiii," they responded in unison.

"Good! She is the one who brought him into the Earth World. She must be the one who will wait for him outside of the qalgiq. She will hold his hand as he walks inside." Sedna sighed. She started to relax. Finally, the welcoming feast could come together.

"Kakoot, Kakoot, what are you doing here?"

It was Mama. He lifted only one eyelid and said to her, "Mama, upirngasaq."

"Kakoot, come home. Imminuuqpug."

"I will Mama, very soon, very, very, soon. Ungaava."

"Pst, Mr. Amos, stop all that shit," came a low whisper. Kakoot opened his eyes to see Wade pulling a wheelchair behind him.

"Now, hop in and I'll show you to my office."

Kakoot flashed a sleepy grin. He pulled himself up and turned around in a full 360, plopping himself into the chair. He looked up at Wade.

"Well, look at you, you show off. Spry old fucker, aren't ya? Now just keep quiet, we got about twenty minutes before anyone comes around looking for you." Kakoot was whisked away down a grey lit hallway.

The office was the broom closet at the end of a skinny, cement tunnel. Wade pulled a cigarette out of a package and handed it to Kakoot. As Kakoot put it into his lips, Wade lit up a fatter cigarette of his own.

"Hey, hey," warned Kakoot.

"Want some weed, Amos?" Wade asked between coughs.

"No, boy, I never did that stuff. Far as that goes, I don't smoke anything."

"But I thought, we shook hands on it—come on Mr. Amos, I might get my ass cracked in half over this."

"Wade, we had an agreement. A gentleman's agreement and we shook hands. I wanted out of that room and you gave me the chance to get out of there. But not like this."

"You fuckin' Indians are all the same."

Kakoot raised his raw brown hand upward, palm facing Wade and said, "I'm not a fuckin' Indian, Wade. Never have been, never will be. But whities get that wrong all the same."

"What are you then? You look like an Indian."

"Inuit. Eskimo. Skeemo. Whatever word whities are using these days."

"You all look the same to me," muttered Wade in disappointment.

"Ditto," replied Kakoot.

With that they both began to chuckle. Slowly, the chuckle swelled into a wave of laughter that washed over the room.

Wiping his eyes, Kakoot looked around the dank room and said, "So this is your office. A cleaning closet. It's the best office a white guy has ever taken me to."

More laughter.

"Now, Wade, I've got to get myself outta here but I don't know how. Can you help?"

Wade took a long pull on the joint and shrugged.

"You know the routine around here, the coming and goings of things—all I need is a simple escape. All I need is to get out. All I need is to be alone."

"How did you get in here anyhow—usually a family member puts you here. Ask them to get you out."

"The government put me here—it's my last stop. I got no family left, Wade. I'm about eighty-four years old and I have no idea where any of my children are anymore. I want to go to the Land of the Dead, that's all. Just help me get there."

Sedna sat up straight. "His bones are starting to feel his tarniq. His bones are telling his body that it is time to move on. I can feel it. Can you?" Sedna turned to the two Old Woman Spirits.

"Aiii," they agreed in unison.

"I do too. I was scared at first when it happened to me. Then the fear left me. Was it like that for you?"

The two Old Woman Spirits hesitated. The oldest among them spoke.

"You just learn to trust your heart in that situation. Learn to let go of it all. All those things on the earth land that tie you up. It's like the feeling you get when we untangle your hair."

"Do you have to bring that up? You old people always have a way of getting back at me!"

"And what do I get outta the deal?" asked Wade. The joint brought a faint glow to the dim room.

Sedna slammed her body into Wade's. "You're high aren't you?"

"Who the fuck are you?" Wade tried to shake his head back to reality.

"I'm the Goddess of all your delusions. Now, buddy, I hear you have an agreement with my man Kakoot. So this is what you're going to do..."

Wade thumped his right palm into Sedna's face and began to run his fingers over her high cheek bones and nose.

"You're sorta hot," he whispered. "You're the best delusion I've had in a long while."

Sedna pushed both palms against Wade's chest. "Back off! You don't want to mess with me. You will serve a purpose today, Mr. Wade. You are the one who will make sure that Kakoot gets to me when I need him to."

"I don't know what they're putting in my weed anymore but..."

"Listen! You get my man out the door and I'll be sure that you're taken care of. You know what I mean?"

Sedna stepped in close to Wade's face and ran a palm down his right cheek. "You don't want to fuck this one up."

"Hey, you got no fingers! How do you, you know, get it on?"

"Listen! Get this in your head. Get him out the door and I'll take care of both of you!"

Sedna ran her oar-shaped hands down the front of Wade's janitor pants.

Sedna paused, "Make sure that you have my man Kakoot back in his room. I'll be waiting for both of you."

Wade grinned while he watched Sedna evaporate part way down the hallway.

Wade turned to Kakoot. "Man, I gotta get you back to your room."

Kakoot was sitting in his bed looking at the clock when the nurse came through the door with her companion.

"Now Mr. Too-Much-Moose, we're taking you down to the main area. We have a real treat for you today—we're having beers!" Again the black bear claws lifted him up from his bed. Again he was slammed into a chair, his head snapping back and falling forward. Again the square white teeth were in his eyes telling him to shut his Skeemo mouth.

As he was being pulled in a long chain of wheelchairs, Kakoot spied Wade in the dining area mopping the sun speckled floor. They caught each other's eyes, and Kakoot nodded at him briefly. Wade nodded back. Again a gentleman's agreement had been sealed.

Along the hand-railed hallway the procession of wheelchair-ridden seniors snaked their way towards the main receiving area. The black man was the lead dog. It was the most singular dog team ever assembled. Pulling their way along the railing with one hand and pushing the wheels of their chairs with the other. An informal death procession.

Wade came close to Kakoot. He bent low and whispered, "Pretend to die. Grab your chest and then I'll come take you outta the line-up." Kakoot again gave a slight nod.

Pull, push, pull, push, pull. "Aaaggghhh!" screamed Kakoot as he slumped into his chair, his hand upon his heart.

Wade looked towards the black man and shouted, "I got it!" but the black man came running anyway.

"That fuckin' Skeemo!" he muttered.

"What's up? He dead?"

Wade said, "Don't sweat it man, I'll take care of it—you got all these other old fuckers to worry about. Here, I'll just take him back over to the nurse."

"Thanks, man—now, I owe you."

Wade pushed Kakoot back towards his room. They were about to enter when along came the nurse. "Now Mr. Loose Tooth—what's wrong with you?" Kakoot did not move. Eyes closed, hand to chest, he breathed shallowly. It was time. Wade lifted him from the wheelchair onto the bed. Kakoot felt himself crossing even as the nurse tried to pull him back.

"Dancers! Drummers! Everyone in place please. Why haven't the Spirit Hunters returned? You, Caribou Spirit, fly around out there and get them back here. Okay, everyone else. This is a test run! Let's get practicing!" Sedna felt the happy glow that welcoming home one of her own always gave her.

Sedna winked. Wade followed her. He could see more women with her but they were a bunch of legs. His own Rockette kick line. They were telling him to hurry up. He obliged.

Sedna smiled. The white boy had done well. He deserved what was coming.

Kakoot walked onto his tundra. It was minus forty with the wind howling in at thirty-five kilometres per hour. He smiled as he felt the tip of his nose go completely numb.

He had made it. White boy Wade had got him home. As bits of snow whipped and bit into his face he removed his hand from his mitt and said, "Sanningajuliuqpaa," making the sign of the cross as he spoke the word.

In the distance he could see all three of his wives. Nobody had aged at all. He called their names into the flat, winter desert. "Pihtwa! Meeka! Saila!" He screamed each name above the wind. Loud. Hard. The women started to jump up and down. He was coming home to them.

He saw her. "Anaana!" Joy flooded his veins. He was her boy again. He was running towards the arms of the woman who had loved him best. His heart filled with happiness, his face smiled with young glee. Dizzy with love he felt his body fall forward, slamming onto the frozen ground.

"Here he comes everyone!" Drums started to beat in a slow rhythm. The Dancing Spirits hopped from one foot to the other with the same thump-thumping. The Singing Spirits broke into song. Kakoot walked into the qalgiq holding his mother's hand. All four of his women were with him. He was home.

Kakoot looked back one last time before the Earth World closed behind him. In the hospital, snow twirled and swirled around a mother and her newborn child. "Kakoot," exclaimed his mom as he let out the first cry from his blue-red mouth. "We'll call him Kakoot!"

ANNIE MUKTUK

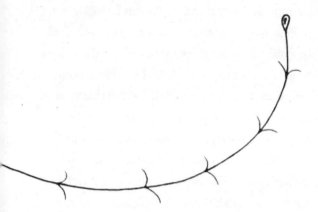

B A I T. There are so many good things to do with it. Slide it onto a fishhook. Put a small amount onto a trap. You can use it in the water and on land. You can put in your freezer and use it in town.

Me and Moses Henry, we're the masters at it. We aren't just best friends and roommates, we are the Master Baiters. No one can out-bait us. We aren't traditional Inuk hunters and fisherman, but we each know how to do that. Our Daddies taught us and we know how to use some of the old ways. We just have a different approach, a different execution. We use our muktuk in other ways.

When the small-framed Igloolik girls come in for some shopping around town we have our bait on hand, thawed and in platters. We put it onto the kitchen table with a tablecloth and then head out. Before we close the door, we each glance back over our left shoulders, grin, look each other in the eyes and whisper, "Bait." It is amazing stuff, it works absolutely every time.

It's fun to hunt for women and the Seaport is the biggest trap you can find. Not a tiny little snare hole, it's a bear-sized trap and the game that strolls through the door are the women. Igloolik women are the best catch of all. They're small and delicious and muktuk is their drug of choice. Tell them you've got muktuk and you've hit a home run, a grand slam.

Tonight was the night. A group of those lovely Inuk bodies had flown in a couple of days ago. Like the husky mutts we are, me and Moses Henry, we were out sniffing the merchandise. It's mostly a new batch this year. A few repeats. Annie Mukluk among them. Moses Henry spied her and started to drool right there in the Northern Store. I punched Moses Henry hard in the ribs for it, told him to quit it. He started to growl and I mean growl. Those Inuit eyes turned to black slits and his lips wrinkled into an O-shape. I thought he'd slam his fist into my face. It's not like we hadn't had our fights along life's way, but really Moses Henry—Annie Mukluk?

What I couldn't get into Moses Henry's head was that she just wasn't Annie Mukluk. She was bipolar. She liked the Arctic and the Antarctic. She played with the penguins and the polar bears. Annie Mukluk liked to fuck and she did it with everyone in Igloolik and everywhere else she went. She'd fuck your father, your sister, all your brothers and finish off with your mother. She swung both ways and sideways.

Moses Henry met her a year ago and still had not forgotten her. She was hot, she was horny, and he appeared to love her. We were the only two over-thirty and under-forty bachelors in town. We had one rule—never love them. We just enjoyed them and moved on. We had a reputation and maintaining it was everything.

I tried only once to talk to him about it. We were out on the land together. She was all he could blubber about; she was his "it." We had strolled along together in our non-traditional hunting gear after hopping off our ATV, looking more like Canadian soldiers in Afghanistan than a couple of Inuk guys tracking caribou. I couldn't stand his whimpering any more.

I said, "Moses Henry, you gotta stop thinking about Annie Mukluk. It's time for you to move on. You know what we all think when you start that crap—you say her name and I hear the jingle, 'Oh Annie Muktuk, what the fuck, who did you screw last night? Oh Annie Muktuk, what the fuck, we know why you ain't tight'." Those words sang their way out of my mouth and the next thing I knew, Moses Henry has drum-danced my ass to the ground.

Bits of twigs are stuck in my head. Moses Henry was a tough son of a bitch, he was fast and could fire a hit to your body quicker than you could blink.

"Johnny, you can't talk like that. I love that woman."

Dragging my arms next to my ribs, I started to heave and peel my body from the earth.

"Moses Henry, everyone from the 58th line up has had her. Not once, not twice but more than three times each. She's the pit stop for all northern jizz. She's the original sperm whale. Don't you get it—she's not your 'it'! She's got a mental disease of some sort, she's weird."

I tried to get that all out before another fist shot out at me. The fist did fly but I dodged it and had a momentary thought of victory. I didn't win. I woke up with Moses Henry's boot holding open my jaw and my right eye was looking into his gun barrel. I heard the slow words, "Take. It. Back." I know one thing about Moses Henry; he means business when he means business. I took it back and for the last eight months I have not uttered Annie Mukluk's name.

Moses Henry has. I hear him in the shower some mornings, saying her name. She has cast a magical love spell on him and he can't find his way out. He sings her name in the most affectionate of ways. When we are out on one of our in-town hunting trips, he searches for her. He compares all the locals to her and I can't stop it. I'll ply him with beer and more beer and he continues to stalk her memory. Annie Mukluk, he won't stop saying it, thinking it and breathing it. Tonight he will be fucking it. All that muktuk on the platter. She'll lick it, she'll suck it and then she'll swallow it. Annie Mukluk, you need to leave Moses Henry's brain.

We are at the Seaport. The jukebox chimes one of my favourite Phil Collins tunes, "In the Air Tonight." That drum solo is the best drum solo. I've got an Igloolik honey on each arm. My, they are fine-boned and for once, shorter than me. Their skin is dark, dark. It's all that seal meat they chew up most of the year. They smile the best smiles and giggle in low tones. Everything they say sounds sexy. It's so hot just being near them. I'm afraid I'll get hard before our dance finishes. I think about stepping into the bathroom for some quick hand relief. As I glance towards my crotch I hear the bar door swing open.

In strolls Annie Mukluk in all her mukiness glory. Tonight she has gone traditional. Her long black hair is wrapped in intu'dlit braids. Only my mom still does that. She's got mukluks, real mukluks on and she's wearing the old-style caribou parka. It must be something her grandma gave her. No one makes that anymore. She's got the faint black eyeliner showing off those brown eyes and to top off her face she's put pretend face tattooing on. We all know it'll wash out tomorrow. She won't look very Padlei in the morning.

Moses Henry is in a state of awe. He is dumbfounded. I feel my uhuk. I look at Moses Henry and a slow smile builds across his face. The room screeches to a stop as Annie Mukluk sashays towards him. She's rolling off her parka. I can see her brown belly button. Someone at the back of the room yells, "Hey look! The arnaluk has scribbled all over her face! Naughty, naughty, naughty!" That corner of the room breaks into drunken chuckles, shoulders shaking in pools of Grey Goose Vodka. I grin but I remember my own anaanatsiaq and the soft tattoo lines on her tender skin. I always thought she was beautiful but, there is no time to remember now. I've got a mission to complete.

Like a war hero from an old black and white movie I leap across the room. I'll put the pin back into this hand grenade. I'll be a local hero. I will have saved Moses Henry's reputation. Landing onto the floor I feel a slap crack across my face. My bottom lip splits open. Blood flosses my lower teeth. I can't believe that bitch had the nerve to do this.

My gut reaction is just that. I reach my fist to Annie Mukluk's perfect face. My knuckle drives hard into the bridge of her nose. Moses Henry snatches my Adam's apple into the palm of his hand. Squirming on the floor I hear, "Say you're sorry. Say it! Take. It. Back!" I can't breathe even though I have a hole in my throat. I can't think. I lay on the floor curled up like the letter 'h'. "Say it, I said!"

Moses Henry, my best friend since residential day school, is giving me orders. I nod. I moan. I swipe the red liquid with the back of my hand.

This is twice in less than a year. This requires revenge— old-style! "I won't say shit to that cunt!" I utter and slowly begin to crawl away. Like a dog with his tail between his legs,

I look back, my head is pointed downwards, but my eyes meet Moses Henry's.

I wake up naked on the kitchen table. The window is open and the white-grey curtains are tugging against the frame. They are gasping deep breaths and exhaling quickly. Another gasp. Another exhale. I realize that it's not the curtains, it's my lungs. God help me. God help me. I roll to the side of the table and vomit up muktuk. Puddles of it. Sour fish smells fill the room. I try to sit up but slump back onto the table. What happened? I can't remember things consecutively.

I remember the Igloolik honeys bringing me home. Take a deep breath. I remember a bottle of Tequila. Take a deep breath. Muktuk in my mouth with a tequila shot. Breathe steady. That's it. That's as far as the night goes. Breathing normally. Trying to sit up again. I'm cold. Need to close the window. I turn over onto my stomach and slide my feet to the floor.

Moses Henry is sitting on a kitchen chair across from me. "You're alive," he says sarcastically.

"Shut the window," I whisper.

"I thought you were dead," he answers, not moving off his chair.

"I'll shut the window," I murmur.

I reach across the kitchen sink. My entire body aches. I look into the sink and puke once more. Turn on the tap. Splash water into my mouth.

"Moses Henry, are you going to kill me?" I ask. I don't have any fight left in me. I don't care if he does kill me. I would take death over this pounding sickness that is in my body right now. I would roll out the welcome mat, sound the trumpets, here I come.

"No." Moses Henry replies. "You're still my best friend. You don't slap a woman. You know better."

"Is she here?" I ask, easing myself onto a chair while wrapping a dish cloth around my balls. For some reason covering them up felt like the right thing to do.

"No, she left with a white guy."

"I'm sorry, Moses Henry," I say, trying to mean it.

It was always like that. The white guy shows up and off goes the Inuk woman. I don't understand the pride that goes with that.

"Guess I learned my lesson," he says. "Guess you were right all along. I'm sorry, too, for the record." He extends a hand across the table. I take it. We have a brief moment of guy love.

"Ah, it's alright," I shrug and grin. "Should we be taking more muktuk out of the freezer for tonight?"

MANISATUQ/
SHE OFFERS HERSELF
PROVOCATIVELY IN
SEXUAL RELATIONS
OPENLY AND WILLINGLY

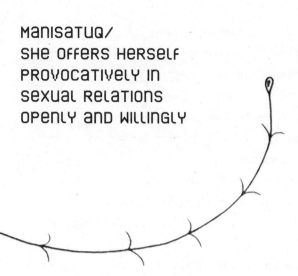

IT HAD BEEN YEARS since I had taken a blow to the nose. Years. Lying on the motel bed staring into the ceiling I remembered the last time a guy had hit me. I was in Grade Four, out on the playground. I ran out first, greeting recess with enthusiasm. I was the fast runner, the female Atanarjuat. I got to the swings before anyone else.

There were only two and I hopped onto one swing and pumped it into the sky. It was all mine until those boys had come along. One grabbed the swing from behind leaving me dangling in the air, legs flailing. The other boy standing at the front commanded me to get off. I looked him in the eyes and told him to fuck off. Big words for a little girl to say.

A little boy's fist smashed into my nose before I could take in my next breath. I slumped forward and fell to the dirt. Followed by the rant of all the little boys I had gone to school with. All of them called me Annie Muktuk instead of Mukluk. They sang long soprano notes of "Annie Muktuk—Baby

Beluga, Baby Bell-ou-gaaa-ou-gaa-ou-gaa" dragging out the letter A. I hated that childhood song. It had changed over to an adult song. "Annie Muktuk what the fuck..." I had heard that one too.

I couldn't stop the songs but I could stop the punching. From Grade Four onwards I thought, this will absolutely never happen again.

It didn't. I had learned how to fight, especially with a boy. Nail his crotch as quick and sudden as I can and I will win. It became my life's most important lesson. It became my mantra.

Growing up I had learned to nail a crotch in a different way. Once I had my hands on their balls, those guys were my putty. I had 'em. Every swing in the world became mine. Men are stupid this way.

"Come on, eh, just move over some." I gave the white guy next to me a gentle shove. The lump wiggled slightly, inching over to his side of the bed.

Ah, these white guys. They like to fuck with Inuk girls. They like to brag about it the way a man comes home from a good hunt. All rosy faced and a belly full of stories. I like the way they look at me, as if I am some precious little stone. I like the chase. The hunt. The first time he puts his palm against my breast. His fingers pinching my nipples and leaving a sweat trail down my spine. The beginning of the fuck is always the best. I let them think they are the leaders. Whoever he is, he gets to be the head goose out in front of my V-shaped crotch. I like to wait to hear their breathing pick up. That first low moan from the back of their throats— Ammpphh. A white man's version of throat singing. Then I take over.

They have become my game. I am always in charge of the hunt. I am always on top. I bend and whisper into their ears, "This train stops when I say it stops." I have them. They can only agree. I give each of them the best orgasms they've ever had. I rarely allow the same interracial ecstasy for myself. After a Matinée Mellow King-sized cigarette, I sit in the stench of our sex and hate them.

There is never morning-after sex. Never the obligatory breakfast together. I sneak out of their beds and back to my own. Never a "good bye" or a "see ya later." Good Inuks never say that. I had learned one thing in my thirty-plus years. Never love them. Fuck 'em slow. Fuck 'em hard. And never fuck 'em again. Sex is the one thing that I do very well. It gives me power. It gives me strength. It brings me a strange comfort.

The white guys are special fun for me. They like to tell me how they are in the North to study. They like to rattle off their credentials. Letters coming from this university or that, sometimes the letters were at the front of their names. Sometimes they droop off their last names. As if any of that matters to me. I just nod and know that they think having sex with me will be some sort of spiritual experience. This is a good game. I whisper a few Inuk words to them and they are in awe. I tell them they have uhuk eyes bathing in quik then grin. My spirit laughs. I can hear the tingling of that laughter after each of them comes.

I give them nicknames based on their performance. I can always tell which one of these white guys is married. Thirty-five seconds of foreplay, six pumps, and a squirt. When that is done, I make them start over because this train only stops when I say it does. "Two Time Louie" or "Three Time Tom,"

"Peak Performance Pete..." Ah, those white boys. I especially like the blond, blue-eyed types. They are easiest and dumbest to snare. Little white rabbit boys who do as directed. Me, Annie Mukluk, I am the CEO of sex. The chief commanding officer and I love it.

People talk but who really cares? One thing about people—they are gonna talk anyways. But this hit to my nose! Who was that guy in the Seaport coming after me in mid-air? It was the swing incident all over again.

"I'm gonna get that little fucker," I mutter. "I'm gonna get him."

Moses Henry had been a fun time for me last year. He was my "Milestone Moses." What a blast he had been in bed. He was fun and funny and he did something that most of them didn't. He considered my orgasms first, before his own. This is what made him most unusual. I had decided last night if there was going to be a repeat in my life it would be Moses Henry.

I had scrambled all over town trying to put together an outfit that would make Moses Henry remember me forever. Bought an old caribou parka from an Elder. Found a washable blue ink pen and went to the hairdressers with an old magazine picture of a woman with intu'dlit braids and a tattooed face. Paid that hairdresser a fortune for those braids and face markings. Walked back through town knowing that everyone was looking at me. And what a grand entrance I had made, right at the drum solo of Phil Collins's best song. It was definitely "comin' in the air" last night.

It had happened so fast. Those square Inuk feet coming towards my face and what perfect timing. What turaaqpuq! Perfect aim! BAM! I got a slap in onto that light tan cheek, though. I didn't mean to crack his lip open. It was a natural reaction. Tucked away inside of us, waiting for us to use them. It's natural. It's real, and it hurts like it's supposed to. After that guy had limped away, Moses Henry had shook his head in slow motion and had told me "No." That's it. That's all he said. "I-want-you-white-boy" was at my side immediately, offering an ice-packed handkerchief for my perfect nose. I had left the Seaport with him and had given him the ride of his life. Anger and adrenalin, the best basic ingredients for sex.

Getting up from the bed, I start to dress. "I-want-you-white-boy" is breathing deeply, lost in his world of books and writings. I know I never want to see him again. He has fulfilled his purpose. I am done with him. Leaving the motel, I head out into the spring air. Crisp, fresh, new. Walking in the stillness of the town, the sound of the odd bark from a local dog. I hear the crackle of the lights. Spring skies are like this, full of colour and dance. The nippy air and the lights are walking me back to my shared room at the Aurora Inn.

I remember being a little girl. The magic that night sky made for me is a warm memory. Sitting on my Mama's lap, we would clap and cheer on the lights. We behaved the way others did at a sporting event. Only us. Together, snug under the lights. I always asked my Mama to stay up all night and we would. Drinking tepid tea, wrapped together like one person under an old blanket, sarliaq. My mom had been the best mom. Every day of my life I miss my mom.

My father was absent, whether by choice or by chance. He was never much to me. He was there, only indifferent. Indifferent to me. Indifferent to my mom. My mom though was everything. We had the best relationship. Always together and ready to cheer each other on. Mama taught me how to cook and sew. How to knit and play siutaujaqtuqpuq—cat's cradle.

"Don't make a mess, Annie, watch for the 'X,' aanauniq."
We would laugh and start over. Mama telling the story, me
watching for the 'X.'

"Aanauniq." Me, I was her "beauty." Strolling through the
streets of town I begin to hum the song of my mom. Every
Inuk had one. Our own pisiit to carry us through life. I inher-
ited my mom's pisiit. It was the greatest gift to leave behind
for me. Better than money. Better than clothes. It's not something you could hang on a wall and Mama's is low and happy.
The lights overhead crackle and skid into one another. I
amble back to my roommates from Igloolik. Cat's cradle and
tepid tea. All those good things.

I look to my right and my Mama is walking next to me. I
am not surprised. She shows up every now and again. Tonight,
we are two high-spirited spirits walking together in the
shadows of the night.

"Mama," I whisper, "I'm all right, you don't need to worry
about me."

"Aanauniq, you need to stop behaving badly around the men."

"Mama, stop. I know what I'm doing. Don't be like this.
Don't tell me that old story again about the woman without
a husband." I hold my head a little higher and strut a little
faster. I can hear the hurried steps of my mother next to me,
scratching at the bit of snow still left over from a hard winter.

She tugs on the old caribou parka, "Aanauniq, you must
settle down. Look at my eyes. Turn your head to me and look
at my eyes."

I stop and bend forward a little and see the eyes that had
first seen me. The eyes that gave me life. The eyes that made
me laugh.

"It's time, my Annie. It's time for you to stop all this
fooling around. You are kidding no one. Not even yourself any

longer. You need to rest your head into the same man's arms each night. It's time, my Annie."

"Mama, I'll try. Here! Take my hand! We'll run together under the lights like when I was a little girl! You know, before all the penises. If we run fast enough we will be able to touch them! Quick Mama, let's go!"

✳ Annie Mukluk runs with her mitt clasped around the hand of the woman who had loved her best. Annie Mukluk runs with her long-dead Mama's hand wrapped into her own.

QUNUTUITTUQ/
ONE WHO NEVER REFUSES
HIS PERSON

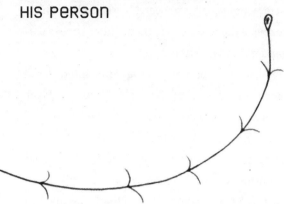

I HAD DEVISED A PLAN in my head. It was all figured out,
how to get those Igloolik honeys to come back to my place.
Of course, the offer of muktuk would remain but I had lain
on this sagging couch for most of the morning building a
formula. My head works this way. I wasn't like Moses Henry.
I had gone to university and studied Math and Sciences
and all things about the earth. I had a BA in Environmental
Science framed and hanging at eye level across from my
toilet. When I'm taking a good, long, satisfying shit I can look
at that degree and grin. Completing a shit was more satisfying than earning a degree. The end result was better too.

I had learned to make numbers spin. I had sat in lectures,
and read books until my eyes were so filled with veins it
looked as though I had been out on a six-week bender. I had
worked hard. I am one of the few and first Inuk guys from my
area to have gone out and completed university. I had loved
the scent of musky libraries and the girls. The girls were so

incredible. They all wanted me. White girls, black girls and every-colour-in-between girls. They wanted to know what it was like to screw some northern meat. I had complied. I had never denied any of them. Wherever they wanted it, they got it. I didn't mind if they were fat or bony.

Eventually I had enlarged a map of the campus and placed small different coloured pins onto all the buildings I had had sex in. The pins were colour-coded: Asian girls, yellow pins. Black girls, black pins. Russian girls, red pins. The colours were endless and the pins clustered into all forms of patterns. At the end of my four years I had sat down and compiled the data. Put together the quantitative and qualitative. Made the charts and graphs and presented it as my final project. I had considered staying on and making it my Master's thesis but that didn't work out.

I know that I am far from stupid. I am a local boy who had gone "out" and stayed "out" for five years. I liked the city. The lights and the pace. The bars and the dancing. I loved all of it. I had returned upon the death of my brother. A death that is never spoken of. I had found myself a nice government job. Got up every day, went for a swim and off to work. I am a regular working guy. I just never saved any money. Who did? Money is for spending. Money is what brings the ladies home.

Moses Henry is still sleeping while I am devising and scheming. I have figured it out. I am going to go over to the Aurora and tell those Igloolik honeys that my shop is open today. Open today for just one thing—washing their hair. When was the last time a guy offered to wash all the out-of-towners' hair? It was my idea. I own it, and I am going to get this show rolling. I am gonna buy some flowery smelling shampoo and line the ladies up. Get out the muktuk. Hit start.

I am going to get laid tonight, not once or twice, but more than three times. And I am going to remember it.

Pulling on my spring boots, the standard green rubbers with spurs, I jingle my way out of the house. I had added the spurs to my boots so I could look different and sound different when I strolled down the streets. I love most the laughter it brings to others. Some days I wear a cowboy hat to go with it. A thick leather belt with my thumbs tucked into it. The jangle of the spurs, with my hat cocked to the side. I am Johnny Cochrane, the northern John Wayne.

"Gonna trap me some polar bears, Pilgrim," I'd say as I tip my hat to the men of the town.

"Life is hard. It's harder if you're stupid" is the quote that I live by. I love being alive. "Johnny Ijuqtajuq"—the name I live by. This afternoon there will be prep required in my kitchen. I have to find one of those sinks that girls lay back into when they get their hair done. There had been a hair salon on every corner in the south. You could cut, colour, and dye all in two hours time but in the North it was razor yourself bald or let it grow to your waist. Hair had no gender partiality above the 58th.

Maggie MacPherson was the only person in town I knew of who owned such a thing. Like me, she had gone "out" and studied hairdressing. She had never stayed current with the new styles though, and everyone had their hair done at her place. All the hair in town remains in a 1980s limbo. Farrah Fawcett or Princess Di dos for the ladies or Bon Jovi-like mullets for the men. I love my mullet. I take extreme pride in it. I like the swishing of it down my back and though my government boss often asked me to cut it I always tell him it's my traditional hair. I am growing it for my people. This is where an Inuk could get away with it. Telling the whites this or that is traditional, required, and needed in order to stay in Eskimo mode.

I ramble up to Maggie's door. Knock politely, take a step back, waiting for the door to open. Maggie appears in her housecoat, a tattered piece of terry towel with coffee stains and various shades of hair dye clinging to it.

"It's a fine spring day, isn't it Maggie?" I begin.

"What do you want, Johnny? I got appointments lined up for today. I don't think I can fit you in."

Maggie is cranky. She's a few years older than me, but I have no childhood memories of her. There was a time, though, when Maggie had been the "Queen of the North." Her days of beauty had faded fast after she had married the local RCMP guy. He had left her after four kids within six years. Her potted belly is wrapped in her torn housecoat and only her bloated tea bag eyes soften her chiselled face. Her faded auburn hair is mixed with grey-black roots and her skinny Arctic crane-like legs hold up the mess in front of me.

"I want your sink Maggie. The one where you can lay back your head. How much for a one day rental on that?"

"My sink! Good grief Johnny—what in hell are you going to do with that?"

"I'm throwing a little party over at me and Moses' place tonight. How about $100?"

"I charge $100 a head in my basement here Johnny. Losing the sink means I lose the business for today. I have four appointments lined up. You can't afford my sink. Get outta here!" Maggie's arm moves to slam the door. The quick jangle of my spur darts into the door frame. I am ready to bargain.

"$600 cash and anything else you want. How's that?" I yell into the crack of the almost open door. The door slowly opens.

"Anything?" asks Maggie, her sagging eyes showing a spark.

"Absolutely anything," I reply.

"Well, Johnny, my kids are with their anaanatsiaq. Do you understand my meaning?" Maggie's sultry voice lowers "Do you understand what I am saying?"

I step into the house. I understand the meaning. I know what Maggie wants and it should only take about twenty minutes of my day. I grin and nod. I understand completely. After all I had been to university.

ITSIGIⱯaa/
LUSTS aFTER IT

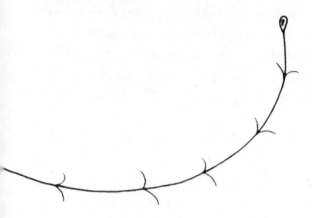

I WAS BATHING. Lying in the bubbles in anticipation of
the evening ahead. Johnny Cochrane had come by and had
invited all the other girls over to his place for a hair-washing
party. He had glared at me and grinned at the others. But I
knew better. Annie Muktuk was not going to miss out on her
last opportunity to have a round with Moses Henry. I was
primping, taking extra care to shave that stubble from my
short, lean legs. My razor rounded my calves and I remembered my night with him a year ago. I leaned back into
the warm water, and closed my eyes. My right hand glided
between my open legs.

"Annie, stop this! Aanauniq! Shame! Stop!"

The back of my head hit the tiled wall and my right heel
slammed against the tap of the bathtub.

"God sakes Mama!" I yelled, "You Shame! You stop! Damn
my heel hurts!" I began to rub my throbbing foot.

"I think I cracked my heel. Fuck it anyhow! What do you want?" I knew better. I knew better than to speak to any Elder this way. I knew that my Mama is my helping spirit. Always on my side, always rooting for me. But I was mad! My foot hurt and my bath time fun had been interrupted.

"Annie, why are you so filled with this sex stuff? Why is it always the men and the thing between their legs that matters most?"

"Mama, why can't you just say it, say, "Penis, cock, uhuk— just say it."

"Annie, my girl, my beauty. We both know it's time. Time to settle. Time to have babies and be like all the other girls. Time to find love and not that other stuff."

"Mama, when will you stop this preaching? Tonight is a big night for me. I'm gonna have him again."

"Him? That Moses character?"

"Yes, him. I like him Mama. I like him a lot."

"Annie, hear your Mama, put these words into your brain. Find love Annie, not the other thing. Uisuppaa."

"You mean make love to him? Not fucking?"

"You always say bad words when you're mad at me. Put the right word into your brain. Uisuppaa."

I stopped rubbing my heel and gave the word some thought. Reaching for the razor from the edge of the tub, I thought about Valentine's Day. I stood up in the bathtub. Took the razor into my right hand and grinned down at my mass of black pubic hair.

INIQTUIGUTI/
THE CAUSE

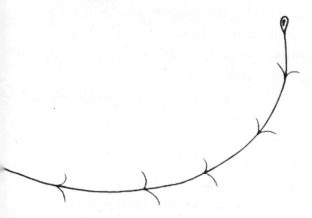

I HAD BEEN DRINKING one night with the Mayor and
mentioned that I thought swimming cured hangovers. He
laughed at me. I kept explaining that swimming released the
hangover toxins. The swim topped off with the steamy sauna
got rid of all of the night before. The Mayor told me that I could
use the pool whenever I wanted to. As he left, he handed me
his keys to the recreational centre saying, "Johnny, you're
gonna need these." Keys and the security code were handed
off and I have swum alone each morning at 5 AM since
Jimmy left.

I love to swim. Since I was a kid, I have loved swimming.
It is one of the things I have done well. I love the feel of
water and the rhythm of my body. Slap, lap, slap, lap. Inhale.
Not too much. Exhale. Gently. Arm straight. Cup hand. Pull
back. Thumb touches thigh. Slap, lap. Hand over the head.
Small breath in. Exhale a little. Keep some air in my lungs.
Something on reserve. Kick. Knees straight. Never bent. Keep

as much of my body as possible on top of the water. Pull
straight back. Only half the mouth out of the water. Inhale.
Turn head into water. Exhale. Kick. Body never lays flat.
Always in a half circle rotation. Slap, lap. Too much splash
means I'm working too hard. Part of my head above the water
or my legs will sink. Slap, lap.

The day after Jimmy was buried, I went to the pool for the
first time since that night with the Mayor. Swimming became
my one focus in a 24-hour time frame. The water is where I
can mourn. My early morning mourning. The chlorine tub
where I fill my goggles with my own sad tears. Some days my
goggles fill up fast. Other days the silent tears for my brother
fill the fog-proof lenses slowly. With my head in the water,
I can moan and scream out my anger. Only the cement floor
hears the screams, and sees my painful face. It watches the
twisted agony of me.

We knew each other's thoughts. Each other's words before
they were spoken. We looked into the mirror of each other's
face every day of our lives. We lived life in a way so different
from those who had been born into this world as singulars.
We were a duo. Jimmy had been a little smaller, a little slower,
but I will never admit it. Jimmy was my brother. When I was
in my twenties my mother confessed her sin to me.

She told me of a New Year's Eve party. A wild group was
together in a trailer, country music was playing loudly
and the Yuk-a-Flux was being shaken and passed around.
Cigarettes and weed, yuk-a-flux and Johnny Cash; there was
no better way to bring in the New Year. My mom would hold
the glass jar of yuk-a-flux on her seven-and-a-half month
swollen belly while the men around her got onto their
knees and would try to lift the jar to their lips, running their
hands around the inside of her thighs. It was their game,

"No-hands-yuk-a-flux." When the clock hit midnight and everyone began to blow into their cardboard horns, my mom lifted the glass jar of yuk-a-flux to her lips. Vodka, fruit juice and melted ice went into her belly and fed into only Jimmy's side of the womb. Jimmy's side of the sack got it. He was born as the FAS twin.

I spent my life protecting Jimmy. At school. At home. It only got harder as Jimmy got older. Our mother drowned her sorrows in Cherry Jack night after night. After I had finished high school, I moved Jimmy in with me. We lived together in the tiny shack of a house until the day I decided I wanted to go "out." Out to the city. Out to university. Out of town before I went out of my mind.

I moved Jimmy back in with our mom. Jimmy had a job then at the port working nights pushing a broom. It gave him purpose and I had wanted to take a break from it all. I told Jimmy how to live while I was away. I promised him letters and gifts if he would just keep going to his job. I promised to live with him again as soon as I had my degree. I had promised Jimmy everything I could think of if it meant I could just get the hell out of the life I had created.

Moses Henry had agreed to check in on Jimmy and I had held him to it. During the next four years I had called Moses Henry at all hours of the day or night asking for full reports. I liked doing this especially when I was drunk. Slurring my questions into the dorm phone, making Moses Henry accountable.

One day the Dean came and got me. Moses Henry told me the worst news. Jimmy was dead. Suicide. Swinging from the side of the dark cement port. I don't remember crawling onto the plane. I don't remember the greeting arms of Moses Henry holding me up while I cried, unable to grab my backpack off the baggage carousel. That was the moment when my life had gone onto autopilot.

I had done only one memorable thing since Jimmy's death. I had gone to an Elder and asked her to tattoo his name on my back in the old way. Thread and soot. The pain of the stitching of Jimmy's name between my shoulder blades had helped my sorrow feel real. Stitch by stitch I would tell myself it would have happened anyway. The medications had always been hard to keep up with and Jimmy had a bad habit of feeling good and stopping the meds entirely. Our mother was useless. Cherry Jack was her daily medication. She had not had one clue what her boy was supposed to take or how.

Some days are tougher than others. Some days I am scared I'll lose Henry Moses like I lost Johnny. And so I swim. The water is the only place that knows my heartache. The water is the only place that accepts my guilt. My regrets. Kiinarlutuq, sad face into the water.

INURQITUQ/
A NICE GUY

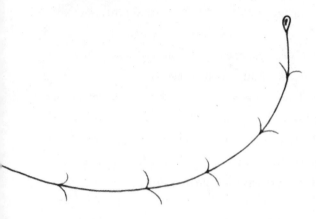

THE SHEETS HAVE WRAPPED ME into a tight cocoon.
My body reeks of Johnny's sweat and vomit. A stench that no
one can fall asleep by. I rerun the night. Hitting replay again
and again.

I could see my breath when I walked through the door.
I thought it was the cold spring air that was chasing me
inside the house. Stamping my feet and removing my jacket,
I could smell the tequila. What a stink, what a horrid smell to
walk into. I thought about turning on the lights but decided
against it. Thought I'd just go to my room and close my eyes
on this night. Forgive and forget. The rule I live by.

When I walked past the kitchen table I saw his body there.
Face down. Drool leaving clear puddles on the floor. Face
towards the open window. I felt my own heart rate accelerate.
Ka-thump-thump-thump. I touched Johnny's back with the
tip of my right index finger. Thumpthumpthumpthump.
Cold. No movement. Thumpthumpthumpthump. No rising of

oxygen into lungs. Thumpthumpthumpthumpthump. What should I do? Who could I call?

Tears spill out of my eyes. "No Johnny! Not this way! Not this way!"

My right index finger traces the tattoo across Johnny's broad shoulders. "Jimmy" is all it says. Plain letters for a plain name. I try hard to take a deep breath but the air won't come. I feel a moan starting to move up my throat. The same sound a downed caribou makes as it clears that last bit of wind from its pipes. The last noise any of us makes. Grief makes us guttural. Grief turns us back into the animals of the land we walk on.

I will not pick up the phone. I can't make that call out to Johnny's mom. I will not be the one to deliver this news. I can only pray. All the memorized prayers of my youth come to my mind. I slump onto the kitchen chair and whisper, "Our Father who art in heaven, Hallowed be thy name, blessed art thou amongst women and blessed is the fruit of thy womb, Holy Mary, Idetestallmysinsbecauseofthinejustpunishments- butmostof all because they offend you my Lord, whoisallgood- deservingofallmylove." The words run together into nonsense. Nothing flows the way it should. My mind is confused. My spirit runs sporadically in circles inside my chest.

Just as I reach for the cordless phone, Johnny Cochrane rolls over.

All I can say is, "I thought you were dead." I didn't show Johnny the absolute joy I felt watching him puke. Inside my heart returns to normal rhythm. The silent words of my prayers fall into line.

"Thank you Lord for letting Johnny live, for letting me be his friend and for giving us both life. Amen." I had wanted to fall to my knees and give thanks but I would never do that in front of Johnny. All I could do was to think "God has granted me one more prayer request where Johnny is concerned."

While Johnny vomited into the kitchen sink, I stood behind him making the sign of the cross. When he was done, we shook hands and we each went off to our separate rooms. Johnny doesn't know that often, while he dreams of pussies and snatches, I stand in his room watching him sleep. I checked on Johnny many times last night. Like a Mama with a newborn. I stayed at Johnny's side throughout last night. Afraid to close my own eyes. Worried that maybe alcohol poisoning could make a return. I held onto to Johnny's strong hand until late this morning. Only then did I allow myself to slide under my own sheets, thinking that today I was definitely going to sleep in. Instead I tossed the events of the night into the air over and over again. Like making a salad.

I feel an overprotectiveness towards Johnny. I see a side to him that Johnny never shows others. The side that cries, feels pain and loss. The side that longs for the identical twin brother. The brother who had been found swinging from a rope on the side of the cement dock at the port. I had been the person Johnny's mom called to go with her to the dock. I had been the one who pulled Johnny's mom away from that blue, battered body, blood frozen to the side of his mouth, empty eyes looking to nowhere, yellow rope carelessly blowing around his neck. I had brought her to my house and picked up the phone to tell my dearest friend to please come home.

TUTSIaPaa/
He asks Him

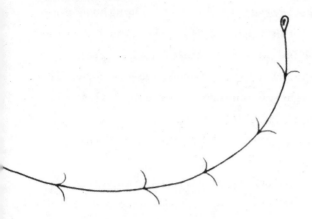

I TELL HIM ABOUT STOPPING OFF at the hotel to ask
the ladies over. Moses Henry's hot on my heels. I'm home
after my swim and personal invitation to the ladies at the
Aurora.

"Did you see her? What did she look like? Was her face
bruised? Was her nose broken? Was she damaged in any way?
What about her hair? Did she still have those hot braids?"

"I didn't see the cunt," I lie, "I didn't invite that horny
bitch over here. I don't need that kind of slut-whore-arna-
lukak over here making a mess of things!"

"Well look at you!" He says. "Busy calling the kettle black.
You with all your women parading in and out of this place
night after night!"

He strides towards his room. "You, you, you—asshole!" he
yells before he slams his bedroom door hard.

As the door swings, I mutter, "Ah, get over it, Moses Henry."
I scream through the door, "Have yourself a good long sulk in

there, you suckie baby! But you better have your cock on by six tonight! That's when our company arrives!"

Geez that guy, can't please him no how. Bring home girls for him night after night and he acts like he's taken a vow of abstinence. God damn him anyhow. What does he see in her? She is pretty and I won't mind having a go at her myself. But how does a guy stick it inside of someone that his best friend has already visited? That's a concept that's just too hard for me to wrap my head around. Some things are off bounds, even for me.

Shaking off that dirty thought I open up my bag of shampoos. There are all sorts of brands inside. Some smell like flowers. Some like fruit. Some have stuff that makes your hair straight, curly, or just shiny. It is a bag filled with tricks and treats. It is the one bag of goodies that no guy on earth should miss out on. The hair party was the best idea I've had since I got home a year ago. Moses Henry doesn't get it though. Ah, he'll come around.

Moses Henry has saved my skinny, brown hide so many times since we were kids. He's taken care of me better than anyone else on earth. I know I owe Moses Henry more than my life. I love him and I'm not ready to give him away like a husky pup to just anyone. Annie Mukluk is the problem.

Annie represents all the things that I fear most. She is the one person who can take Moses Henry away from me. Moses Henry has to realize that Annie Mukluk can only be a fling. An annual event. Something to be enjoyed and discarded, like fireworks on Canada Day. Moses Henry saying that he loves her only makes a mess of things. I am Moses Henry's isut-sipaaq, his lead dog pulling Moses Henry's life to where it should be. I plan on staying in first.

I find the only tablecloth in the house and fluff it onto the table. The silver platter from on top of the fridge is placed in the centre. I remove the muktuk from the freezer and put it onto the oval disc. I do all this tenderly and begin to go through my collection of CDs. Start out with Eddie Rabbit, who would be lovin' the rainy night and keeping it going until Phil sings me home. Ah, the food, the mood, and now the waiting of a night of recreation.

Lying back down onto the wilting couch I fall into a light snooze. "He'll get over it," I say to no one in particular. "He always does."

Nakuusiaq/
A Love Gift Received

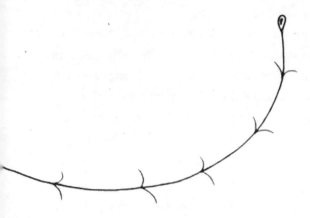

SIX O'CLOCK and the ladies are arriving. Light knocks at the door and Johnny is off the couch and bounding to the entrance like a dog chasing his own tail. He is wearing only his underwear. So excited. Ah, these Igloolik girls. They are standing on our step, a small group of six. Giggling like a gaggle of geese. Johnny is happy, the kind of happiness that makes your toes tingle. The kind of happiness you feel when you're a Christmas morning kid and that one gift is possibly under the tree. Sarimajuq.

I saunter out of my bedroom door. My eyes fall to disappointment realizing that she is not here. My mouth moves into a straight line. I pull back my hair and say, "Welcome, ladies."

Johnny smiles at me. He thinks I'm getting over it. His happy face bobbing up and down at me.

The night begins. Johnny is the maestro of this orchestra. He is the front man to this pussy pit. He has the wand that will create an evening of magic.

Resigned and re-assigned I return to my bedroom to get elastics for my hair. Turning to leave, I hear a light tapping on my bedroom window. My tundra swan is looking at me. Her nose is swollen and dark shadows circle her beautiful eyes. There is no Padlei on her face tonight. Only her long dark hair and a smile that looks painful. I slam my bedroom door and open the window. My Annie struggles to wiggle her body through it.

"You're here," I whisper, "You're here! Look at you. So beautiful."

Annie Mukluk tries to stand to her full five-foot-two frame but her foot is aching so very much. Her body is lopsided. Her face is bruised. Her nose is the size of a soft ball. Her small weight feels like an anchor as she stumbles into my arms. She is my broken woman.

"What happened? What's wrong?" I ask as I lift her.

"Hurt my foot in the tub. And this face," says Annie pointing to the bulge above her upper lip, "that's courtesy of your pal Johnny."

"I am sorry for all this Annie. I am. I just wish…"

Annie places a hand on each side of my face, "Imaa. We are together now. Usiqtuq."

"Here, put your foot on a pillow. I'll get ice for it and we'll just visit. How's that?" I want her to feel better. I cannot believe that she is here with me, in my room with me. Right now.

"No, no, don't leave me, Moses. I have a gift for you. If you can just help me take my pants off."

I am receiving the invitation of a lifetime. I happily unbutton Annie's Levis. We both listen and watch as the metal zipper slides open ceremoniously. I can't do anything but stare. It is that feeling we get when we know we shouldn't look at something, but can't stop ourselves. It is the knowing of something better to come. Something we can stop but don't. The spilling of thousands of lined-up dominoes and the sense of satisfaction that comes with watching them all fall in perfect order.

I stare at my heart-shaped gift. I love it. I love her. Johnny will hate this.

Phil Collins and the Igloolik girls sing, "Take me home" while I bend and tenderly kiss my Annie.

Johnny Cochrane dances in his underwear in the middle of the Igloolik circle, singing, "take me home."

Annie Mukluk's mother's spirit fades from the corner of the room.

This was where things should be and should stay. Piujuq. Saimmavuq.

QANINNGILIVUQ/
HE GOES INTO THE DISTANCE

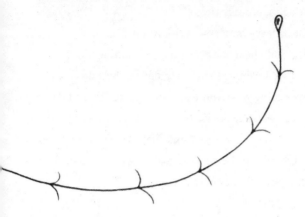

"I'M MOVING UP TO IGLOOLIK," I announce. I can't
stop staring into my coffee cup.

The apartment is in a shambles. Lacy black underpants
dangle from a light shade. Beer bottles are scattered all over
the floor. Bras in various colours and shapes lay on the back of
the kitchen chair I am sitting at.

"Yeah," replies Johnny. Johnny is back on the sagging
couch. Laying naked with a cloth over his forehead and one
over his crotch.

"What are you gonna do up there?" asks Johnny. Johnny
thinks this is another one of my passing fantasies. The one
where I become a preacher.

"They're looking for a pastor up that way, thought I'd go up
and see what it's about."

"So, you're not moving. You're gonna go and smell around
up there—right?"

"Nope."

Johnny struggles to sit up.

"God, hangover days get harder and harder. This must be part of the aging process, right?"

"I'm gonna leave tomorrow. With Annie Mukluk."

"I wish I could hear you correctly. Let's start again. You're leaving tomorrow. You're going to Igloolik to be a preacher—again. You're going with Annie Mukluk. Moses Henry, take your life off repeat. The preacher hooks up with a whore and goes out and saves the world? Think that one has been done." I can feel the anger in Johnny's throat. He is now a naked soldier sitting at full attention.

"I love her," I tell him.

"Everyone loves her, Moses Henry—absolutely everyone!"

I lift my eyes from my coffee cup and look directly at Johnny. There is no anger in this room, only an eerie kind of peace that I know Johnny can't understand. Can't put his finger on.

"I love her," I repeat, "and yes, we are going to ride off into the sunset together and live happily ever after."

I smile and ask, "What about you, what are you going to do, Johnny Cochrane?"

"You know Moses Henry, I've been thinking of heading off back south. I didn't tell you but I applied for the Masters Program at U of M. Got the letter yesterday. Been accepted. Thought I'd start with a few courses this spring and just take it from there."

Silence blends in with the smell of stale beer, nicotine and sweat.

"Hmph," I snort, "Guess we both had plan B's happening."

Johnny stands and wraps the cloth around his head like a bandana. His crotch cloth falls to the floor.

"Yeah, I guess we did." Johnny coughs and shrugs.

"Let me get cleaned up and we'll go out and do one final thing together. Alright?"

I smile and nod 'yes'. I'll always be Johnny's lead dog.

samaGiiK/
TWO WHO CaLL
eaCH OTHeR PaL

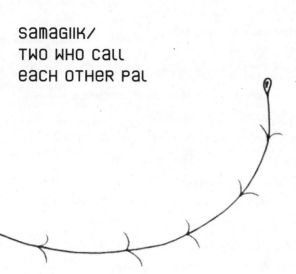

"WHERE IN HELL ARE YOU TAKING ME?" Moses
Henry is squished into the ATV sidecar next to me. We have
been bouncing across the land for over one hour. Bobbing
around the Hudson's Bay like a pair of baby seals. The shore
line is craggy and the ice is starting to soften. Spring ice is not
to be messed with. Basic Inuit 101. Don't fuck with the floes.

"Johnny! For God's sakes man—where the hell are we going?"

"We're almost there," I grin and scream, "Don't be a suckie
baby! Preachers don't look good when they whine." I turn
back and hit the throttle a little harder.

"Fuck man!" yells Moses Henry.

"Now that's not good preacher talk, Moses Henry," I yell
back while I make a quick left.

I jerk the machine to a stop. Both of our bodies lurch
forward.

"You're gonna kill me so I can't leave! I knew it! There are
times when I absolutely fucking hate you, Johnny Cochrane!

Look at where we are," screams Moses Henry, "right in the middle of fucking nowhere!"

"This is a place where me and Jimmy used to come. That's his grave over there." I say back to Moses Henry in a whisper. I point my chin towards a small hill.

"Johnny, Jimmy's grave is in town. In the graveyard."

"No. I moved him out here. Come on. Follow me."

"You moved him. You can't move bodies around, Johnny! I think there's a law against it. It's not like a coffin is a friggin' salt and pepper shaker or something."

"Oh, look at the preacher giving me a sermon. Preach on, Moses Henry. Preach on, Preach." I start my cackling laugh. Like the old ravens that hang around town. The laugh Moses Henry has heard all his lifetime. The laugh that makes him happy because this is how Moses Henry knows when Johnny is happy. Moses Henry decides to let it all go and just enjoy the moment. One of his last with Johnny.

"When did you bring him up here?" asks Moses Henry.

"About a week after the funeral. My mom wasn't gonna get him. She gets his headstone and she can think he's under all that but I brought him back to where he and I fished and hunted and smoked dope together for the first time."

"You smoked weed with your handicapped brother. Jesus, Johnny!"

"Ah, only a couple of times. It was fun for him. Anyway I brought him back to our playground. Our private playground."

Me and Moses Henry stand over the pile of rocks. The grave of Jimmy. I lean forward and pull a foot long, die-cast white corvette from the front of my snow pants. I look over and smirk at Moses Henry.

"Almost as long as my penis, eh!" After a bit my laugh lines straighten and the corners of my eyes moisten.

"He always wanted one of these. Found it on eBay last week. Had it flown here. Thought I'd leave him something to play with while I'm gone. Can you just say one quick prayer over him for me, Moses Henry? Something nice."

Moses Henry closes his eyes. Bows his head and begins:

"Our dear Lord, times change, people change and together Johnny and I ask that you keep watch over our Jimmy. We're both heading out in the morning, Lord. We're both moving on. We ask that you keep Jimmy safe and secure in the loving palms of Your hands and we ask more that Johnny and I will live our lives in a way that is honourable to both You and Jimmy. May both of your spirits never leave either of us. May the love we both felt from Jimmy always remain a part of who we are and mostly Lord, protect Johnny here as he swings down south to study 'cause I'm sure going to miss him. In your most precious name Jesus. Amen." Both men automatically make the sign of the cross.

Johnny wraps his arms tight around Moses Henry's neck and sobs.

"I love you Moses Henry," Johnny manages to say between wet tears.

"I love you, Johnny," replies Moses Henry. "Let's go home and pack."

HUSKY

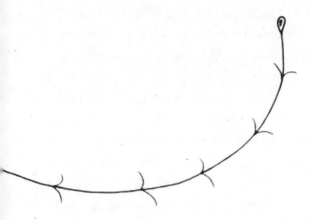

*Cecil "Husky" Harris, the HBC Factor at Poorfish Lake on
the edge of the tundra, had three Inuit wives at the same time
and even visited Winnipeg with them all in tow, staying at
the Empire, then known as the Husdon's Bay Hotel. "Harris'
wives were quite a mixed lot," reported his colleague Sydney A.
Keighley. "One was old and ugly, one was young and pretty,
and one was short and very homely."*

— PETER C. NEWMAN, *Merchant Princes*

BITTER COLD. Spring wind singing an aria outside, and
inside my little cabin, a fire is crackling us through the night.
I often sit up and look at all of them, spread out like sled dogs
across the wooden floor, sleeping. Wondering how my life had
become this tangled mess. I'm one of them now. The other
trappers even call me "Husky."

I came here to make my fortune and I have a bit of money tucked away in a mattress. Money. Paper with other peoples' faces on it. It is useless up here. Something to pull out and look at, count and put away. The shadow of the fire flutters pirouettes across their faces. I indulge the beauty and innocence that sleep gives—especially to them. Knowing they are off in their dream worlds they soon will awaken from and share with me. Telling me of what they saw, what it meant and what the future will hold. I never stop being amazed by the stock they put into their night visions. No matter how large or small it is, it is all interpreted with awe and reverence. It is part of being Inuit. I decided that long ago. They live their lives close to the ground. I won't stop it.

I light my small pipe and pull on the handle with my lips. I'd had a good life in Nova Scotia. I had gone to school, learned to read and write real good—Mama wanted me to go to Dalhousie College. The ad in the local paper caught my eye and I thought it would be grand to head north. I became a company man, an HBC Factor at this tiny post. It is my job to mingle with the locals, to barter for their furs and to learn their language. Maybe I had taken it all a little too far though. First one wife and then another and another. Oh, how my Mama would keel over and squeal over it, if she saw what I was doing. Well, the Bible does say, "A man shall take a wife..." The 'a' part would be disputed, singular as it is. Like Shaharaim in Chronicles I may never have a son until I get rid of a couple of them.

The trouble is, I enjoy these women. Each is different and each arrived at my post with a different story, a different reason for staying on. In time we formed an unconventional family in the white world. In the world of the North, this kind of living arrangement is the norm. They each came with the intent of leaving but never did. I used to wonder if they would leave, but now our lives are meshed together in such a web that it is as though they were always here. Perhaps this is the life that I was always supposed to have.

The babies start to be born, our lives becoming knitted up tighter. I am the Papa to three different and beautiful little girls. Each a different mom, each a little bit different looking from the other. They are my girls, the extension of me in this cold, northern world. I taught them some English but mostly they all speak their moms' tongue and so do I. When I learned their language, I began to respect their culture and it became a part of me. It moved into my heart and set up camp in my soul. It became who I am.

I'm rocking on this creaky old chair and thinking of all that money. Money from the company. Money from my own trapping. White fox and wolves, their hides have stacked up and so has the money. It is time to go somewhere to spend it all. Time to take off for a while before the winter decides to really settle in. Time to take this qatangutigiit south.

There are times when I long for the white life. For tea to be poured into porcelain. To hear the sound of motorcars. To know I can stop at a pub for a quick brew. I miss the brew. The company sends some in at Christmas, but this is such a small post. We are poor in supplies and low in the things that matter most—brew and smoke. Tobacco is rare and I bring in enough to plug my pipe every evening. The brew is sipped at until late March. This is something I never share.

Yes siree, it's time to take this group of ladies into the city. They can take in the sights and the sounds and see the white life. I get excited just thinking of it all. I'll take them to the big Hudson's Bay store down on Portage Avenue. We'll have the time of our lives. I chuckle to myself as my chair carries my imagination away to concrete sidewalks and women with lipstick.

Sometimes I pine for the company of a white woman, even though I've got these three. The pretty one, her name is Tetuk. Her father traded her for a can of Macdonald tobacco and a box of bullets. How could I say no to her beauty? All my Christian upbringing left me when I looked at her. She came to me when she was around sixteen. For three winters now she has done nothing but given me a ton of boners and one baby girl. Her hair shines, her eyes grin; it excites me to think of her. There are no boundaries in bed with her. She howls and growls and sits on my belly, rocking back and forth, licking all of me. Those white women back home would never do this. White women only get onto their knees in church, I chuckle to myself. Our baby girl is three winters old.

Alaq is ugly. I have never seen her with teeth. Lips are worn from chewing caribou hide, cheekbones are dug high into her face and her tiny black eyes peek out from their sockets like a baby bird's. She's smart and knows what I want before I say it. She knows what I want, period, and never refuses me, no matter what time of day or year it is. She's the type who gets the job done, not always quickly but definitely efficiently. She showed up one day all alone. Said she had been travelling for a couple of weeks. That was two summers ago. Our little girl is one spring old.

Keenaq is oldest, softest. She is the calmest. Filled with patience. She likes the slow movement of sex. She likes things to last. She takes the longest and slowest way when it counts. She is quietest and speaks only when she thinks it matters. She understands the wind better than the others. Understands the seasons better. She's a good trapper too—lots of Arctic hare. Keenaq left her group after her husband died.

She didn't want to go to another man from that bunch, so she walked into my cabin on a stormy night and said this is where she was staying. Our baby daughter is one summer old.

These women take care of every part of me. I would be a lost man without them. We've had all the seasons with each other and they are always at my side in some form. Keenaq checks the trapline with me. Alaq makes all my clothes. Tetuk has to do only one thing—be pretty, and she's good at that. I never give them to the other white men who stop by to trade. This is something else I never share.

Those other assholes don't understand it. They laugh at me and call me "Husky," tell me I've crossed over and can't come back. They'll fuck the Natives but they won't stay with them. Say they'll burn in hell if they get too involved. But they come here and see my settled life and I know a part of them is just jealous. Here I am, twenty-four years old, the husband of three Esquimaux women and the father of three babies. And there they all lie before me on the floor of this cabin. Life really could not be better except for my itch to take them out. I want them to see the south. The other side of what I know. We can paddle our way to Nueltin and from there fly out to Churchill and take the two-day train trip into Winnipeg. It'll be our spring vacation. It'll be the time of their lives.

✳ Next day I say to my ladies, "Ikauqpuq" as I load the canoe. They seem to think we are going to go out to get some supplies. I tell them we have a long trip and to get ready. They load the boat with only the things they can carry. I estimate three long portages between here and Nueltin. These women know how to travel light and scramble up and down the lakeshore to the cabin in three trips each. We are off, babies are tucked into each mother's amaq and away we go. I am excited and together we paddle away from our tiny HBC log home. The wind is light, the blackflies are buzzing, and we sing the only English travel song I've ever taught them.

What do you do with a drunken sailor?
What do you do with a drunken sailor?
What do you do with a drunken sailor
Earl—y in the moorrnnning?

Shave his balls with a rusty razor!
Shave his balls with a rusty razor!
Shave his balls with a rusty razor!
Earl—y in the moorrnnning.

Our spirits are soaring high above the tiny whitecaps of Poorfish Lake as we paddle our way towards what is called "civilization." It takes us five sleeps to finally make it to Churchill. Another two on the train ride down south. My ladies are forlorn. They don't like the plane—they scream, the babies scream, and I scream at them. My wives tell me the flying friends of the bird-man once married to Sedna have returned and the plane will dive into the waters below and we will all be killed. The flying friends are pounding their wings and this is why the plane bumps and pushes the clouds around. Their stories arrive at the worst of times.

They whisper it to each other as our plane hits turbulence over and over again. Their faces tilt in fear and the babies dangle from their hoods like so much glue. No matter what I say they won't listen. I know it's wrong for me to yell at them but the plane engine is chugging out loud. It grunts and groans and I can't help myself. These are women who never raise their voices. Screaming is their way of telling me of the terror that lies inside of them.

I try to tell them that this is like riding on the bumpy tundra on our qamutikkut—the sky is the land upside down. This doesn't work. It is a terrible trip—the pilot asks us to never ride his float plane again.

The train ride jostles them too much and my daughters cry and cry and cry. My wives sit with their heads hiding behind their summer caribou hoods. I can only do one thing. Go to the bar car and enjoy the brew. I am drunk for thirty-six hours straight. It is the only way to manage this vacation. We finally arrive in Winnipeg and the worst hangover of my life has nested into my head.

I manage to load us up into a taxi and my ladies look exhausted. The babies have fallen into unconsciousness after all their crying. My wives need to have a bath. My head pounds and all I want to do is lie down. Off we go to the St. James Hotel. The clerk at the front desk doesn't know what to do with us. Her eyes become owl-round and her words stumble out of her mouth.

"Yes sir? What would you like?" says the pretty blonde lady with the red, red, mouth. Fear is drawing straight lines around the edges of her lips.

My women circle close to her. Alaq touches the clerk's hand and holds her red nails close to her eyes. Her small nostrils flare as she tries to smell the polish. Tetuk bends low to the floor and is running her hand around the black stiletto heels of the clerk. She pushes her body away from the woman and lays her head on the floor. She pulls a small stone out from her sleeve and rolls it between the heel and the base of the black shoe. She is grinning, thinking she has made a new game. Keenaq is pressing the clerk's yellow hair in her both of her hands. She is smiling and saying in a low cooing voice, "Aumajuq, aumajuq."

A high-pitched scream sounds. A man in a dark suit is throwing us out the door. We are thrown onto the street like a barrel of chimps. The babies cry—again.

"Fuck you!" I scream to the gent in the dark suit. "You fuckin' whities—fuck you!" and I make a fist. My women cower together, hiding their eyes behind their hoods.

"You and your fucking Indians aren't welcome here, asshole! Get those fuckin' savages away from the streets—Now!" The heavy door slams in our faces.

"We need to find a room! Look what you all did! Got us kicked out! Now what?"

Tetuk stands on the tips of her toes, puts a hand to her hip, smiling. Alaq rubs spit onto her fingertips, rubbing it into her fingernails. Keenaq throws back her hood, dividing both sides of her hair into her hands. They all burst into the biggest laugh I've heard in eight days. They each chatter about the white woman at the desk. They are saying she is only good for one thing—how could a woman who looks like that have any skills to stay alive? They gather up the three babies and walk alongside of me with a giggle that lasts for ten city blocks.

❋ We walk single file into the Hudson's Bay Hotel. I'm a Factor—they can't refuse me. The baby girls are tired and their mothers are still gossiping about the woman at the St. James desk. I turn and give them the nod. They quietly shuffle to a corner.

Behind the desk is a company man. Young, bright blue eyes, flaming red beard. When he opens his mouth to speak the stench of stale whisky fills the air. This is a man I can relate to.

"Me and my girls need a room, Scottie—how much for a couple of nights?" I grin at this young fella and he grins back.

"You and the blackies in the corner? A hundred bucks for two nights."

"Hey, hey, hey, I'm the Factor at Poorfish—give me the company rate."

"Blackies leave skid marks on the sheets—fifty bucks a night—no negotiating."

"How much of it lands into your pockets?"

"About sixty bucks. But there's not another soul for miles and miles who'll give you a room, Factor—not another soul."

I reach into my pockets for the paper that will get us into a room, onto a bed, into a bathtub.

"Here you go, Scottie—thank you most kindly." I lean in to shake his thick hand and as we clasp palms, I quickly make a fist and say, "Listen you little Scottish asshole, I'll get my extra sixty bucks back one way or another! Got it,—ya little red prick?" My teeth are gritted and we have one small moment where I see fright building in his pupils. I've got him scared and that's all that matters. I'm small but I'm tough. I've wrestled with all kinds of animals in my time. This little red prick is easy prey.

I turn to my women, wink, and nod, saying with a smile, "Attagu!" They all grin back at me and off we go up the stairs to room number one.

There are two beds and the babies are removed from their Mamas' hoods and rolled onto their sides. My tiny girls look like tiny cigars in a tiny cigar package, bundled up tight in their brown caribou skins. I head to the bathroom and turn the water on for a bath. All my wives stand behind me, peering over my shoulder and saying how good it is to make water flow inside. I step away from the tub and let them know that they are first.

I didn't expect them to all get in at once, but they did. What a time they are having, splashing around and laughing. I stretch out on the other bed, cradling my head in my hands. Thinking how happy I am to be here and to lie down after days of travel. I let out a long yawn and look towards the bathroom door as it opens. Keenaq is smiling her wise smile, her dripping body floats towards me, her weathered-brown hand stretched out. I look at her and grin and she pulls me up from the bed. Together we walk towards the bathroom. Our eyes dancing with each other.

As I crouch down into the already grey water, my ladies shrink to small Sednas. They are little women, like the little people, as they wiggle over my belly. I can only see the tiny shadows of them because of all the steam inside this room. I can only feel their hands, their tongues and their toes waving over me in the most sensual of ways. I moan and groan and try to catch them as they dash over my body. They have become minnows of what they are normally. This spell that is over me is too lovely to swim my way out of. It feels like a drowning dream but I'm drowning in the sound of my own short breaths, the feel of their tongues around my balls and I can't stop it. I think I can hear the sound of two of them throat singing. The sound of nature's noise.

Tetuk crawls on top of me. She is the size of a one-foot china doll and we fall into waves of perfect rhythm with one another. I scream my pleasure out to the dripping walls. This has to be a dream. There is no other man on this earth who would believe what is happening. I believe there is no other man on this earth who has had this form of pleasure. I can only go with what is happening around me. I can only let these small fish-ladies have their way with all of me.

I open my eyes to an empty room with all the water drained from the tub. Where are they? Alaq arrives with a towel wrapped around her worn body. She takes it off and hands it over to me. Have I made all this up? She looks at me with her hollow mouth and asks, "Nakuusiaq?" I nod, understanding the word but not really knowing what has just happened. She nods her wrinkled face and says in her best English, "It is good," as she leaves the bathroom.

This is the mystery of living with these ladies. The things that happen when I am with them I don't understand. The things I try never to think too hard about because there is no way of putting into words what has just happened. It is these kind of times that I find myself filled with the secrets of these peoples and I only know that I have to keep these secrets locked away inside of me. There is no one to tell them to.

When I walk into the main part of the room, my ladies all smile at me. They each have one of my babies on their laps and we all begin to sing, "What do you do with a drunken sailor..." It is the happiest of afternoons.

✳ Keegan McTaggart stands in the boiler room, boiling over. That bastard, he thinks, I'll get that son of a bitch. I was in the North once, I know what those little Factor pricks are all about—I'll beat the little fucker blue before he leaves town. Sixty bucks, that's my money—it'll help to get me back home to Kilwinning. Back to my màthair. I'll go back into the coal mines forever if it means I can be back home.

Taking a swig from his bottle of Birch's Black whisky, he swallows hard and shakes his head. These Canadian Bay men, he thinks, these dumb arses, I'd like to wring every one of their lily white necks. I despise those fuckers. The way they boss all the rest of us around as if we are their servants. They've got no loyalty, no morals, no sense of right from wrong. What kind of man would match hisself up with women like that? You gotta have some pride man. Not be running your prick up every northern hole! I've told myself too many a time now, Keep the heid! Keep the heid!— well I'm good and damn tired of keeping that heid and I'm gonna do something about this time. He'll not get his sixty back and I'll be damn sure of it!

Listen to the circus goin' on up there. I can hear 'em. Moanin' and groanin', screwin' and sweatin' and then cacklin' out songs about it like a bunch of wounded geese. Mother of God, they're the worst bunch that's ever walked through these doors. Shame on that Husky—three of them for himself and proud of it! That man will surely rot in hell—surely!

Those short little men been pushin' me around this town too long—I'll wait for him and then I'll get him with my slim-line pocket knife. Three inches of steel was all a man ever needed to do any real harm and shadows are made for getting even.

✳ My ladies are shiny-faced and smiling as we strut into the Hudson's Bay Store. We all head off to the ladies department first. They each find new dresses made of cotton and kerchiefs for their heads. The colours are dazzling—blues and yellows and reds. We find flat shoes in the shoe department and off we go to buy nail polish and lipstick. I pull all that paper out of my pocket and proudly pay for my ladies' new clothes. They look magnificent and stunning. In all of this colour, they almost look white.

Off we march to the children's department and find small denim trousers for the little girls and fluffy dresses with buckled shoes. I pull all that paper out of my pocket again and give the sales lady at the counter what she wants. The baby girls are giggling and making happy screech noises as we head out of the children's department and to the toy department. We buy one tricycle and three dolls with yellow hair and blue eyes. The baby girls are cooing over their babies as we head to the men's department.

I find a black suit with padded shoulders and wide-legged pants and bright white shoes. My ladies purr in approval, with low growls from the backs of their throats. I feel like a king with his court of lovely ladies as we all leave the store with our new clothes on and our old clothes tucked away in big bags with HBC printed on them. All of our shoes click down the sidewalk, the sound of new footwear echoing around the streets of Winnipeg. It's a sound my ladies have never heard before. They take turns stopping and walking and laughing as each of them struts or walks slowly down the sidewalk. They each keep their heads down, watching each footstep to see whether it is their own or someone else's. At last they hold hands with each other and the baby girls and we walk together in on large horizontal line on the sidewalk, clicking our tongues in unison with the concrete. I put my oldest daughter onto the tricycle and slide her down the concrete. The rhythm of squishy wheels and high-pitched giggles bring the best of smiles to my face.

The sun warms the new garments on our backs and I know it is time to find something for us all to eat. We clamber into the Hudson's Bay Hotel and find seats in the small restaurant. Along comes the Scot, Mr. Keegan, to take our order. He is a scowling young man today.

"Keegan, my friend," I say, "What's the lunch special today?"

Keegan glares down at me from his square built height. His hair and eyes look the same furious red. The stubby fingers on his right hand are forming a fist.

"Read the bloody chalkboard ya skinny little Eskimo fucker!"

Keegan is one spitball of flame today. I don't want anything to ruin this day. This was our day, our day of shopping and laughing and clicking around in new shoes. My ladies have their heads down. The loud Scots-punctuated tongue has frightened them. My three little girls sit together with their bottom lips trembling.

"Frighten my family, will ya? Ya dumb Scot. Over-charge me on my room too—ya bloody piece of Scottish shit. Here's something to get your ass humming!"

I grab the little fucker by the flickering sparks of his scraggly beard and twist my body around him in a vertical half-nelson. I got him bent from the waist down, slam his forehead into the empty table next to us. Forks, spoons and knives twirl and sputter against the hard wood floor.

"I'll just keep banging your potato head against the table until I hear the magic words, 'I'm sorry, Sir Husky'—ya got it?" It takes all the force I have in my chest to hold Keegan's cube-shaped body in this position. I just can't stop.

"I'll bang your fuckin' initials into this table with your fucking forehead!"

Rage has filled my veins, flowing fast and hard into every part of my body. I want to kill the little fucker.

I feel a sharp punch to the back of one of my knees. My body slopes over to one side like the skis of my dogsled on a hard turn. I feel my head whipping backwards and slam against the floor. I can hear the ladies screaming and the howls of my baby girls as the hardest work boot lands into my balls. All the air in my lungs hurdles forward and runs across the floor in leaps. I can't suck any wind back into my chest. All I see are gritted, square teeth speckled with blood break into as smile as the shimmer from a pointed piece of silver dives into my right eye.

I hear my own screams dance in circles around them. It grips onto the tiny hands of my little girls and swirls them into a jig with the deep groans of my ladies. Together all these sounds break into a reel, dancing together the hurt of each of us at once.

✴ Across the room a blurry picture of King George V and a tall, breasty white woman with a crown on her head next to him. I stare at them as I reach my hand up to my face and feel a mushy balloon on my right cheek. The soft, rough squares of gauze tickle my fingertips and I move my swollen right index finger in search of my nose and mouth. I find them, large and blubbery. I take a deep breath, relieved to find they are still on the map of my skull.

I ache everywhere. Moving my finger down my body I try to feel my balls. I find them chilling on a bag of small ice chips and for some odd reason this is the funniest thing I know. I laugh and chuckle and air sputters out of my lungs along with half-formed whimpers. The memory of Keegan's black work boot hits me hard—again. I don't remember much afterwards, only that something glittered and later gutted my eye socket. I smell the sterility of the hospital room and feel anger rise up into my fists. I look back at King George V and remember why I went North to begin with. Life in the south always ended with you trapped in a hospital room.

I swing both my legs over the edge of the bed and steady myself against the thin mattress. I have to get out of this place. This is where white people die. I have to get out of here. I manage to find a chair to slide across the floor to guide me to the tiny brown closet. Just get my pants and shirt on and I'm outta here. Just open the closet door and reach in and get those pants and my shirt. Just sit on the chair now while I get my feet inside my pants. Just take it slow and easy and stay calm. Just...

"Mr. Husky—you'll not be doin' any form of escapin' on my watch!" A woman bigger than the one with the crown in the picture is squeezing me by the shoulders. Her large hands are dug deep within my collarbone and I can't move. I feel like I've been ambushed by a polar bear. Her mouth is large, her lips are black and her teeth are jagged as her head sways close to mine. Her yellow eyes are fierce. I am being lifted and thrown back onto my skinny bed. My head is cushioned by the pillows behind me. I cannot think of one word to say.

"You old trappers. Ya come into the city and get yourselves liquored up and beat up and then wind up here for me to look after ya. Damn you all!" Her words are less than an inch from my face as she roars into my left ear.

"You'll NOT and I repeat, NOT, be sneakin' out of this room when I'm on duty. I've had one too many a doctor blame me for you types leavin' in the middle of treatment. Not let your bodies mend inside these walls. Aye, Mr. Husky—you're not leavin' today!" She steps back from me and reaches to close the window.

"I'm gettin' the doctor in here right smartly, Mister, and he'll talk some sense into ya. In the meantime, I'm gettin' you something for the pain and makin' it strong enough to keep you inside these walls until my shift ends!" The polar bear sways out of the room. Her big, round paws are almost silent on the floor. Her head nods as she walks away and her ass jiggles with a sense of purpose. I am too terrified to move.

Seconds zoom past me and the polar bear is back. She has a large spear in one of her paws and she is moving her face close to mine. Her nose is flaring and those teeth are pointing at me. I turn my head as I feel the spear stab into the crook of my left elbow. The room spins into a whirlpool and I hold tight onto either side of my antiseptic bed. The polar she-bear holds both of my hands and moves her nose close to mine. She is swinging her head from side to side, the way I know they do before they pounce on their prey. I grit my teeth hard and form the biggest ball of spit I can, rolling my tongue into circles over and over again and then I shoot it from my mouth like a rocket ball from a Winchester. I see the she-bear howl and her head snaps up like an arrow, pointed edge up. My body lifts from the bed and I hear my back snap in a loud crack. I feel my body tumble into nightfall, the sky black, the stars shining. I relax as I float through the air.

✳ Keegan stands in front of the group of women who've been left behind.

"Too bad old Father McGinty came along, I'm thinking. Too bad he broke up our fight just when I was getting it started. Now what's gonna happen to you? Look at ya. All gussied up like white girls. Nice shoes. Nice dresses. Nice kerchiefs wrapped about your black, dumb heads. Maybe it's time for you to know what a real man is." Keegan steps back and grins at each of the ladies. They bow their heads and whisper to one another.

"You'll stop it!" Keegan yowls, "You'll stop it, ya hear!" He yanks Tetuk's baby girl from her and holds the little one close to his chest. The tiny girl begins to cry as Keegan holds the slim-line three-inch pocket knife close to her throat.

"Which one of ya is the mother to this one?" Keegan yells. "I say, which one of ya is the mother to this little black female bastard child?"

Tetuk steps forward, head down, eyes staring into the black boots that knocked Husky breathless.

Keegan moves forward, pulling Tetuk's kerchief-wrapped hair from the middle of her head. "Well, lookie here, you're almost pretty. Better than the other two nags ya got with ya!" He shoves Tetuk's baby girl onto the floor and gives her a small punt with his black boots.

"You oldies, over there—you take this kid back and get up to your room. Me and this one are headin' downstairs for a little real man fun." Keegan siezes Tetuk by the scruff of her neck, swings open the door to the boiler room and pushes her down the stairs.

Tetuk's frightened eyes bolt to Alaq and Keenaq. She utters one firm command, "Tapiriik!" as the door slams shut.

Alaq and Keenaq hear the lock of the door click as Tetuk screams.

Alaq and Keenaq gather up the baby girls and fly up the stairs to room number one. They lay each of the little trembling bodies beside one another on one of the beds. Keenaq licks the tips of her fingers and begins to rub and blow into the eyes of each child. In seconds the trembling stops and the little bodies soften with calmness. Alaq reaches around each tiny neck and pinches the base of each skull. In seconds the tiny girls are sleeping, their tiny breaths are rhythmically slow and steady.

Keenaq and Alaq change their clothes. They are back inside their summer caribou robes, their hoods are pulled low, almost touching their chins. Keenaq reaches inside her sleeve and pulls out a small bag made of potato sackcloth closed up with a piece of twine. Alaq pulls her hunting knife from her left sleeve. They look at one another for one quick moment and head out the door of room number one. Keenaq looks to Alaq at the top of the stairs and yells, "Inuttapuq Kajuq!"

❋ Tetuk cowers in a dark corner. Fear has taken over every part of her body. She is unable to stand straight as Keegan runs his square fingers down the front of her blue dress. He cups her face in his hand as Tetuk slumps against the concrete wall. Keegan reaches into the pocket of her new dress.

"Well, lookie here! What I've found—red lipstick!" Keegan hands it to Tetuk and tells her to put it on. "Paint up your brown face for me a little, will ya!" Keegan points towards a cracked mirror next to his bunk in the boiler room.

Tetuk stands in front of the mirror, her hands shivering with fear. She moves the red colour around her quaking mouth.

Keegan bursts out laughing. The sound of his laughter darts in circles around the hot basement.

"Ya look like a clown from the circus—yes ya do! More— put more red stuff around your mouth!" Keegan demands. "More—because I'm running all of me into that hole and I want it to look like a real woman's mouth!"

Tetuk turns towards the mirror once more and slowly rubs the red colour around her lips. She reaches into her pocket and pulls out an eyeliner pencil. She draws in the traditional beauty lines onto her chin and cheekbones while Keegan pulls back the one blanket on his wooden cot. With each skinny line, Tetuk feels her spirit strengthen. Power is returning to her soul.

✳ Keenaq and Alaq work the lock on the door of the boiler room. Alaq silently wiggles the lock with her hunting knife while Keenaq stands back, her head down, the words of her prayer flooding the room. She prays for the strength they are each going to need and for the situation to be handled quickly. She prays for the little girls upstairs. Prays that they will not awaken with fear. She prays for Alaq to slice the lock on the door the same way she has seen her skin a fox or rabbit—only one smooth cut.

Alaq nods a low grunt and the door is carefully opened. Keenaq and Alaq stand together; Keenaq unties the small potato sack and throws the contents high into the air. She holds tight onto Alaq's right hand and they both jump as high as they can underneath the sprinkling of moss and twigs and other natural magical things from their tundra. They soar together to a ceiling beam and look towards one another. Sitting across from one another is a Raven and a Snowy Owl.

✳ I'm so sick of just lying here. I wish the doc would come by. It feels like I've been here since forever. I hate the smell of this place. I got to get out of here. My fuckin' head pounds.

These are the only thoughts that come to me while I am lying on my bony mattress. I miss our little cabin by the lake up North. I miss the simple things—the fire glowing all day long, the sound of birds passing through. I miss building my own traps and hearing my little girls coo with their moms. It was a mistake. My mistake. Bringing us all into the city so I could show off. That's all it really is—just me and my male pride. Me wanting them to see what else the world has to offer. In the end the offerings are pretty slim.

"Well, here you are, Mr. Husky! I'm Doctor McGrady. Ya got yourself into a fine pickle haven't ya!"

In my left eye I see a young, dark-haired man. Curly hair, gold-wired glasses dangling off the tip of his pointed nose. He's wearing a long white coat and all I can wonder is how old this kid is. I wonder if he's ever got his dick wet. I sigh and know I have to behave.

"I'd shake your hand, Doc but I can't reach out that far. Tell me about my eye?"

"Your eye will heal up with one hell of an ugly scar. The blade fractured your *os spenoidale* and a smaller fracture to the *os lacrimale."*

"What's that in English?"

"Here and here." Doc McGrady points to his skull on either side of his right eye.

"And your sorry nuts will eventually drop back to normal, but for the next long while you'll need to just get yourself onto the mend. Lots of rest and relaxation. I hope you don't mind but I don't see any reason to keep you. You're staying at the HBC Hotel?" McGrady peers over his swaying rims. I feel like I'm under inspection. I have to be good.

"Yes. Me and my family."

"Your family? Now I've heard about your pack. I understand you have three Native women and three little halfies to boot. Is this the truth?"

"It is, sir. It is. I was just thinking that I'm sorry we ever came down this way—should have stayed up home is what we should have done."

Doctor McGrady smiles and says, "Now Mr. Husky, don't you be frettin' for bringin' the ladies down to our end of things. It's good for them to see the other side and good for your wee ones too. What I'm going do is leave some pain medicine at the nurses' station for you to take back home with you. Just a moment." McGrady leans out the doorway calling out, "Nurse Agatha! Nurse Agatha."

In strolls polar she-bear. She's round and rolling towards Doctor McGrady, her yellow eyes are smirking, her tongue swinging like the pendulum of a grandfather clock. I feel my good eye start to twitch as the muscles in both legs begin to cramp. If I could run, I would. Faster than any Arctic hare. I'd zig-zag my way to safety. Agatha—the name suits her just fine.

"Nurse Agatha, I understand Mr. Husky has been under your care exclusively over the past day or so. You've done a fine job."

I snort. Both heads turn towards me. I pretend to cough, place one hand on my chest and wave the other in the air explaining that I'm OK. Inside my heart pounds. I would like to take this woman out to a back alley, straighten her arm out and run as much morphine as possible into her veins. This bitch is trouble.

"I'm leaving some pain pills at the main desk for Mr. Husky to take back home. Please be sure he gets them and also, help him get his clothes on. Remember all patients are rolled out in a wheelchair."

"No. No," I protest. "That's fine, Doc. I'll put my pants and shirt on by myself and I'm sure I can walk out of here."

Polar she-bears rumbles a low growl.

"Well, how about this—I stay back and supervise you getting dressed and walk you out myself. You're quite a legend around these parts, Mr. Husky. I'd appreciate lending a hand to you."

"Well, thank you so much, Doctor McGrady. I'll be happy to leave."

"I'm pleased to have been of some help to you, Mr. Husky. I'll brag about treating you to all the other doctors who didn't want to take you on as their patient. You're one hell of a tough son-of-a-gun. They tell me you shot a polar bear from your bed inside a boat one night. Is that true?"

Polar she-bear stands erect, full height. Her paws clawing the air. Her nostrils burst into round bubbles on either side of her mouth.

"Sure as hell is, Doc. It sure as hell is." I stare back at polar she-bear. She stands down. Her shoulders slump and her eyes drop to the floor.

"I don't know which one of us was more surprised, me or that bear, but I got her lying across my fireplace at home. You're welcome to come by and visit her one day."

Doctor McGrady laughs and extends his hand. "You're one of kind, Mr. Husky. Just one of a kind. That's all for you, Nurse Agatha. Resume the care of the others on this ward."

McGrady and I clasp hands like two long-lost pals while Nurse Agatha waddles from the room.

✳ Tetuk is looking traditional. Her face is marked with the beauty lines only the Inuit use. She is feeling strong now. She is powered up and ready for anything Keegan would like. Her body is not shivering any longer. She's ready to play this game once and for all. She is ready to take on this red-headed Scotsman. She is going to win.

"What's this shit all over your face?"

Tetuk smiles and leans in close to Keegan's face. She lets her tongue roll around her mouth, tasting the plastic of the red lipstick. Keegan grins.

"Well, we're all beautiful when our eyes are closed, aren't we?" says Keegan. Tetuk unbuckles his belt and the only sound in the room is the soft zip from his fly. Tetuk's eyes hold steady with Keegan's.

"Now you're talkin'," whispers Keegan. Tetuk's small hand dives beneath Keegan's scratchy underwear.

"Noo jist haud on!" shouts Keegan.

Tetuk stops. Her eyes ask a question to Keegan.

"You're movin' too quick now! I'm the one in command down here! Got that!" Keegan's broad hand swoops hard and fast across Tetuk's face. As the sound of the smack rings out so does one other small, singular, sound: "Hoooot."

Keegan looks towards the beam of the boiler room. There sits one lone owl, eyes unblinking, black pupils glaring.

"What in God's earth is that thing doin' in here?" Keegan pulls on Tetuk's arm and shoves her onto the bed, reaching for a broom at the same time. As he stands on the edge of the wooden frame, a raven swoops from behind, plucking a small clump of red curls.

"Youch! What the fuck?" Keegan jumps from the bed frame in time to duck the claws of the Snowy Owl.

"My Gawd—it's a nightmare!" screams Keegan as the Raven swoops towards him. He darts again. The owl flaps its wings onto the bedpost. Keegan turns around in time to see Tetuk's feet flee up the stairs.

"Get back here ya bitch! Ya, fuckers—now look what you've gone and done!"

Raven lets loose a furious "Caw."

"I'm not afraid of ya!" Keegan screams. "Not afraid!" He swings the broom above his head in circles, like a batter up to the plate.

"I'll get ya both. Ya daft birds!" Keegan takes the stance of a pro baseball player, the broom his mighty bat.

"Come on! Come at me! Hit 'em where they ain't!"

Raven comes at him like a deuce, curving hard to the right. Keegan steps back once and lifts his eyes to the ceiling, "Can't catch me, can ya? Ya stupid bird!" He touches the dusty floor with the tip of his broom. "Give me another!"

Snowy Owl glides towards Keegan, in a straight, soft line. Keegan leans in hard towards Snowy Owl and puts all his weight behind the broom. Snowy Owl sails past him and sits on the edge of his bed.

"Thought you'd play some chin music for me," Keegan grins. "Well, that's strike one only."

Raven sails through the air like a dart.

"You're comin' right down Broadway, Mr. Raven!" Keegan swings hard. The dirt on the floor forms a Tasmanian Devil dance.

"Huh, only one left to go and I guess I'm out!" Keegan shakes his shoulders. "You're next, Mr. Owl—you're next and I'm gonna smash that head of yours hard. Twin Killing time!"

Snowy Owl lopes towards Keegan. The room has moved into slow motion and the screams begin. Raven is sitting on Keegan's head, her claws sinking into his skull. Keegan's pores are small geysers of blood-red shooting towards the ceiling, spigots on full. Snowy Owl sits on Keegan's left shoulder, wrapping both broad wings in circles over his eyes. Keegan's hard screams become slow whimpers. The hum of the boiler room chugs along as always.

✳ "Tetuk. Thank God you're here!" Husky reaches out for his most beautiful wife and hugs her close to his chest.

"I've missed ya," he murmurs into her hair. "Missed all of ya so very much." He can't stop holding her and together they rock back and forth.

Husky forces himself to step back from Tetuk, "Turqavik?" He asks and nods at the same time. Tetuk nods and smiles back. Shouts of happiness ricochet around the room like a stone skipping across still water. Alaq and Keenaq close the boiler room door and join the circle hug.

Alaq tucks a tuft of red hair into her pocket, "Iksarikpuq!" she exclaims with a happy smile.

"Husky" Harris was a trapper, an H B C Factor at Poorfish Lake, and a man who assimilated "backwards" from non-Inuit to Inuit life. He died while still serving that historic company. Husky is a man I only know about from stories and snippets, for Husky was also my grandfather.

This account is just part of what may have happened on that glorious trip, a time of fun, and a time of family for Husky, but a time of shame for the H B C company men like Keighley. This story examines the representation of Inuit women outside of the tundra and as an Inuk woman and writer, I believe that many of these representations remain alive today.

MY SISTERS AND I

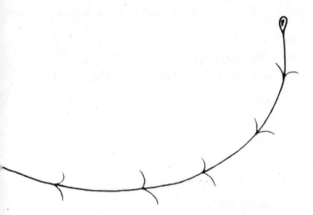

1

I look into the sky and see the geese returning. A smile creeps
up onto my face. I know that soon my sisters and I will gather
the down and eat the eggs, warm from the nest. I will feel the
hot yolk slither and slide down my throat and into my belly.
It brings great happiness to my heart. I know that there will
be cheerfulness in my tiny camp. My camp, with my three
mothers and father and sisters.

The air is fresh with spring. The smell of ice lingers
in it but that does not dampen my spirits. I return from
my morning outing, the moving of bladder and bowels.
Contented and excited for the new season. Winter can feel
like forever and this past winter has been long.

The snows had come, all kinds of it, but we had managed.
My father had found things for us to eat even though the
caribou had not run. We lived on everything we could find
and had survived.

We aren't like the others of our kind. We don't even live with them. We go to the others only in times of starvation. In times of hunger, otherwise we stay out on the land. On our own. People come to us instead. We have visitors and the mothers love having company drop in for a few nights. All kinds of people come. Even white men. Men with different coloured beards. They are trappers. People from far away who think they can make some of that thing called "money." It is made of paper and sometimes shiny rocks. I have never understood it. It means nothing to me.

I understand the times of work and play. The times of getting up early in the day to gather what is needed. To melt snow to water. To get tiny bits of wood in the spring. To eat what is brought to me. Boiled and warm or raw and cold. I understand the sky and all it holds. The moon, the stars and what they mean to each other. I know what it is like to be hungry and and to be full and to work on hides to make clothes.

Today the sky is full of geese returning from their winter home. Welcoming friends who have been away for a season. It is like a homecoming of people who have been lost from one another. It is today. Today is all anyone has. Today is all that ever mattered. To think of more than today is wrong.

I bend into the tent and whisper into one of my sister's ears, "Uvunngapuq." My sister, older, rounder and lazier than me, continues to sleep.

"Sister, come see," I whisper, "Come see! The birds! They are here with us!"

Puhuliak rolls over, looks at me and says, "Go back to sleep. The sun is not even here yet."

How can anyone sleep through such an event?

"Sister, come. Come see them. Come say 'tunngahugit'."

Puhuliak grins, her eyes making tiny angler lines even when they are closed.

"Not me. I won't." I know that she means it. Never can she be awakened. Sleep is her friend. A friend she spends a lot of time with.

Hikwa has overheard the good news. She sits up from beneath her caribou robe. She stretches her arms. Hikwa is different from Puhuliak. She is small and lean. She loves to move at all times. Always busy. Always going. Never still. In one quick move, she darts from beneath the robes. Pulls her skin boots to the top of her knees and grabs my hand. I love this most about Hikwa. I love that she will do anything at any time. Our mothers say that Sister Hikwa is not altogether in this world. She lives in another place most of the time. I don't believe that. Hikwa is the most fun person I have ever known. Hikwa can see and understand what others can't. The mothers may say that she doesn't live in this world but I know that Hikwa is a shaman. She has special powers. She has special strengths.

Together we giggle across the tundra. Today we are one with the geese.

The geese circle above, and we call back to them, "Aruk, aruk." From above the geese see two tiny dots flapping their arms in unison. They see two little girls rolling on the small willowed hills.

The happiness of the morning lingers as the sun peeks into their world.

2

It always stops there. My dream. I never get to see the rest of that day. It happened. I remember it still as I sit here in this place. This place filled with rules. The white people call it a school. My father said we had to come here. All three of us. Why? That's the part I never understand, why he sent us away from him. This place is different. We sleep off the ground. We have all been given strange names. Names that make no sense. Names that make me feel different. I don't know who I am anymore.

They speak French and English here. I don't know what French is. I only nod when I am asked something. Puhuliak is now called Suzanne. Hikwa is Margarite. I am Therese. Once we were, Puhuliak, Hikwa and Angavidiak. Now we are these other girls.

The women here wear long robes made of light cloth. Qallunaaqtaq. They make us wear the same thing, only our robes are short. They put cold, hard coverings on our feet and tell us they are "shoes." We drink water from under the ground, filled in a brown wooden circle. We sit at a table, in chairs that hurt my back. The food is white like these people. It's like filling your mouth with clouds. Swallowing quickly means I can leave the table sooner.

What is hardest is that I can't talk to my sisters unless I speak in French or English. If the long robes hear me speak to them the way I always did, they beat me with a strip of hide. Papa did that to the dogs when they were bad. Hitting them with tigaut, the hardest part of any whip. Sometimes they will reach into our mouths and pull hard on our tongues. It is their way of telling us not to talk our language.

That hurts. Everything here hurts. We have to live our days the way they want us to. We don't go outside. I watch the world from inside at my school desk and remember what it was like to live with my mothers and father. I remember the smell of air that was a part of my every breath. I remember eating when I was hungry not when a clock told me to. I remember playing the string game with my sisters whenever I wanted to. No one ever told me that a round, black dial was my avasirngulik. My elder would not act like that thing.

That's a new word for me, "time." In this place everyone is on time. At home the sky told us what to do and when. I nod and try to do what they say. Sometimes they smile but most times they frown. I talk with my eyes. They talk with their lips.

I am not allowed to sleep by my sisters. We have to stay off the ground on separate wooden frames. None of this makes sense in my head. I look forward to each night to dream of what I miss. Dreaming of what I knew best, of what was only mine. I smell the caribou and feel its soft skin around my shoulders. I see my mothers smiling at me at night. I long for them. Their crinkling eyes. Their fingertips tenderly tickling on my shoulders. I even long for him. My father. The man who sent us to this place.

Suzanne whispers to me often that if we are good we will leave. We will go home. Every day she tells me these same words, "Be good. Nod your head. We will go home. Upaluajaqpuq, obey well." Every day it doesn't happen but I do what Suzanne says. She's the oldest. She knows best. Margarite is different. She doesn't nod her head. She sticks out her tongue when the long robes aren't watching. She makes her eyes wide and points her finger pretending to be like them. She folds her hands together and looks to the ground while she walks behind them. Wiggling her behind in wide, long circles.

I am the one who gets caught. I am the one who gets the strip of hard hide across my hands when I laugh at what my sister is doing. I get put into a bare room. It's cold and dark and smells like rotten willows. I have to stay there for a long time some days. I can hear the food people when I am there.

I can hear the banging of pots and pans. I tap my fingers to their beat and whisper a throat song, "Aii, Aii, Aii, yah, yah, yah..." It brings me to home for a short time. Margarite has been put into this dark room too, she likes it though. She says she sees home. She talks like Igjugarjuk, the angakkug who sees visions. When we can sneak our time together she tells me she saw what our mothers and father were doing. She tells me their conversations and how they miss us too.

One day Margarite and I hide under some stairs at the back of the school and she tells me everything she sees. She makes me remember what we were and tells me what we will be. She says that soon we will fly home. She says that we are like the sisters of Kadlu, the three of us. We will get home. Our parents really didn't lock us out like Kadlu's parents did. Margarite is like Tootega for me. She is wisest and I believe she can walk on the water. I am in the middle of the sisters. I have to listen to both of them. I try my best to be what the robes want us to be too. It's hard. Very hard.

There are many robes here. Some are men and some are women. We never see the hair of the women. I would like to know what is underneath their coverings. They each wear long beads with a cross on their necks. Their leader wears the biggest cross. Some of them have round see-through circles in front of their eyes. Their eyes make me think of Issitoq, the flying giant eye who has the right to punish me. I fear those man robes more than the others. They are the ones who will punish me most. The men in robes all have beards. They talk in quiet, deep voices and ask about us three. It is as if we are too different from the rest. We are never supposed to be together. We are never supposed to sit together for meals or sleep near each other. The robes say this is for the best. This is the way we will learn to be something that will make us better than what we started out being. They tell us about this God and how he is watching over us. They tell us if we don't behave we will be covered in fire. Their stories make me tremble. Suzanne tells me that we have to respect their stories. We have to listen to what they tell us. She is oldest and wisest. I try to obey her.

Margarite laughs at their stories. She thinks they are funny and tells me that they are only trying to make us do what the clock wants. She tells me that the clock is really their God. She makes funny sounds, mixing tick-tock noises with the songs our mothers taught us. It makes me giggle and Margarite even makes this clock song when we are in the classroom.

Then the robes pull her hair tightly and she kicks and laughs as they lift her from her desk with one fist full of the hair from the top of her head. Margarite calls them names we would never speak out loud at home. Holding her up above the floor they spin her around. Her hair twists and twists but she never screams. Her red face sings our throat songs from home while they curse her for breaking their white taboo. They tell her that she is going to go to the place of fire. They take her from the classroom and put her into the room stinking of dead willows. I get jealous. She is going home again for today. I have to stay in this room and learn to write with a wooden twig. I have to learn about numbers and small words. I want to go home with Margarite. She will fly away from the stinky room. She will see and hear what I can't. I wish I was with her just for today.

Suzanne is the opposite. She sits straight. She learns how to move the twig across the yellow empty paper. The robes like her best. They tell her that she is going to go far in this place. But where is there to go? There are three floors. There is nowhere else to go to. Suzanne doesn't understand. She says if we do as we are told we will get to go home. I keep my head down, my eyes to the floor and I remember the day of Margarite and I hearing the geese fly to us. It makes me feel good. I never look at the robes unless they pull my chin up towards them. I don't want to see them with their clear round glass shaped eyes. I don't want to know about them.

3

One night Margarite comes to me. She had spent all day in the willow room. She sneaks to my wooden frame one night and tells me that she has a plan. We are going to run away! Far away from this place. In the moonlit room I can see her puffy eyes. Her mouth is cracked open and there is blood on her forehead. I put my finger into my mouth to wet it like our mothers used to do. I reach out in silence, nodding. I place my finger on her face. I nod once more and I see the tears spill from her eyes. I whisper only "ii" because yes, I can feel the excitement of leaving this place. I softly rub my finger around her eyes and across her swollen lips, "ii," I whisper again. We briefly touch noses before Margarite crawls back to her wooden frame. Now I have a plan. Now I have a purpose.

I cannot sleep for the rest of the night. I am too excited. I trust Margarite to get us out of here. The next day dawns as always. There is the clanging of a loud metal ball inside a piece of steel that has an igloo-shape. It shouts to us before the sun is awake. It is our boss too. It tells us to get up, get dressed and to make our wooden frames look flat. We gather into one line like we are one half of a flock of geese. We go to the place where the water is in white bowls. One bowl for our faces. One bowl for everything else. We line up again and go to the chair place. We stand behind our chairs. The oldest long robe tells us to put our hands together. We look at the floor and wait for her to finish the words. Then we say "Amen," and sit in our hard chairs. We wait until everyone has the grey, thick slop put into their dish and pick up our metal sticks. We chew and swallow at the same time. The old robe claps her hands. We stand behind our chairs. Again we bend our heads and she says words and ends with a song about, "Our Father." We walk like stick geese to the classroom and sit again in hard chairs for the rest of the day.

Today Margarite is behind me in our walk to the classroom. The old robe and one young robe stop in the hallway to whisper to each other. They turn their backs to us and it is then that Margarite tugs on my cloth dress, puts her other hand around my mouth and pushes me in the room of rotten willows. I blink at her in the darkness and she has her finger by her lips. "Shh, shh," she hisses. I stand still, starting to tremble. I will wait for her to tell me what to do. We hear the sound of hard shoes getting smaller and once there is silence Margarite nods.

I run behind her not making one sound. It is like when we are out gathering eggs on our tundra. I pretend I am there and I try to tiptoe as I run. We are sneaking up on the ptarmigan. We are going to swoop our hands under their behinds and lift them. We will snatch the egg before the bird knows what has happened.

I tell myself to be swift and stay closer to Margarite. Before I know it we have run out of the rotten room and down the stairs. We are nearing the back door. The sunlight feels warm through the window. It is now that I can sense it. It is now that I feel the giddiness of freedom pump out of my heart and into my head. Freedom is everywhere inside of me. It is in my eyes. It makes my fingers tingle and I can feel laughter spewing up my throat. I am going to be free!

Together we push the door open. We are outside! We are free from the robes. The rotten room. The hard chairs. The wooden frames. We are together clasping our hands, we break into our own laughter and spin around and around and around. For that very small amount of time I know that I am who I was born to be. I am Angavidiak. I am free!

I hear the sound of geese off in the distance as a bearded black robe snatches me up into the air.

I twist and twist myself in small half circles trying to see Hikwa. The beard has his waxy hand over my flattened lips. I chomp down hard on his skinny, wormy fingers. I hear him gasp as he lifts his hand from my mouth and slaps it hard against my right ear. I don't care.

"Ajujuq Hikwa!" I scream from deep inside. The wormy hand hits my left ear. Ringing wind swirls around me, it's all I can hear.

Sister Mary Rose is chasing Hikwa. Hikwa is laughing and laughing. She is darting around like a rabbit. No circles, only jagged rabbit prints. Hikwa is good at this. She is fast. It's a game we played at home. The white whip hand slams hard into the back of my head. I feel my body thudding to the cold earth.

4

My eyes try to adjust to the willow room.

"Hikwa?" I ask. "Hikwa?" I see the small streams of dust-filled light coming from the bottom of the heavy wooden door. I try to stand but my head and hips hurt. My finger-tips can't feel anything from the cold in this room. I run the palms of my hands over my head hoping they will show me if I have any bumps. My eyes are puffy. My ears are swollen. My lips have ballooned into one giant lump. My nose is the smallest point on my head.

I hear the heavy key clanging against the big door. I scrape my body along the floor trying to get as far away from it as I can. The outline of Father LePage stands in front of me. Today he is my giant.

"Therese," he states, "Sister Mary Rose and I are here to help you. Now stand up!"

I can only stare at them. I can't stand up. My legs won't let me.

"Therese, stand!" Sister Mary Rose straddles herself over me and lifts me up. I wobble the way newborn caribou do. I feel dizzy. The willow room spins in large circles around me. Sister Mary Rose scoops her elbows under my armpits. I take a big breath of air.

"Hikwa?"

"Your sister? This is what you ask for—your sister! You should be asking for forgiveness, young lady," Father LePage sighs. He turns to the robe. "These animals, these so-called children, they will never get it correct."

Father LePage places his long nose in front of mine. "Your Hikwa, your sister is doing penance as will you!"

Spinning his head towards Sister Mary Rose he demands, "Clean her up a bit and bring her to my office." Father LePage leaves the willow room, his keys clanging with his fading footsteps. My body slumps against Sister Mary Rose.

Sister Mary Rose whispers things to me as she washes my face. I don't know her words. I know they are soft. I don't have to be scared. I know she will not hurt me. The coarse cloth runs rings of warmth gently over my cheeks and ears. Sister

Mary Rose says over and over, "Don't be afraid." Words I will tell myself for the rest of my life.

We walk down the dim hallway together but we don't touch. I don't want to touch Sister Mary Rose. Instead, I want to hold tight to her and ask her to take me home. I want to hide under her long black skirts and wrap my body around her knees. I tell myself her words. I whisper to myself, "Don't be afraid."

We enter a room with more chairs and a big table. Father LePage is sitting in a tall chair. I see Hikwa in a small chair. I try to run to her but Sister Mary Rose pinches my shoulder. Hikwa turns her face to me. Her tongue is clamped between two pieces of wood. She cannot speak. Her hands are lying on her lap wrapped in a brown rope that snakes its way around her ankles.

"Your sister, Margarite, is learning the power of silence. Would you like to learn this as well?" Father LePage asks.

I glance at Hikwa. She signals the word "No" to me with her eyes. A slight turn of her head showing me the pain she is feeling.

I feel the tears dripping from my eyes. All I want is to touch Hikwa. I want to feel her hand in mine. I want to know that she is there under all the bruises and black spots on her face. I lower my eyes to the floor.

"I said, Therese, do you want to learn the power of silence?"

Father LePage is standing in front of me. I feel his hand slice into the roots of my hair, my head snapping up, his nose close to mine. I can smell the breath of a white man. It smells like nothing I know.

His lips are tight, drawing a thin line over his yellow teeth. I reach my own tongue into the back of my throat and shoot a bullet of spit onto them. I hear Hikwa's high-pitched happy moan.

The power of silence has entered the room. Father LePage is choking. He spits onto the floor and walks towards his table.

"Bring her here!" he shouts.

He slams me into his tall chair and reaches into my mouth. His long white fingers search for my tongue. I make my tongue dance in my mouth. Hikwa is gasping giggles across from me.

Father LePage stops bobbing for my tongue. He takes one quick step towards Hikwa and slaps her head hard with his big, black book. Her body rattles and shakes in the chair. Her head rests on her chest. Sister Mary Rose steps towards her but Father LePage screams, "Back! Back!"

He reaches into his table drawer and brings out two small pieces of wood. "Like skinning a cat!" he screams as his hand darts into my mouth.

The pain from the wooden clamp. A clothes peg on my tongue is the most pain I have felt since being here. Father LePage wraps my hands in the same brown rope as Hikwa's. I look to Sister Mary Rose and see fear covering her face. He binds the rope around my feet and takes one step back.

"Look, Sister," he exclaims, "I've created twins. My own Helen and Clytemnestra! Twin animals learning the power of silence! They'll not dare to speak again—their language or ours!"

The pain is starting to turn the room black as Father LePage slides Hikwa's chair against mine.

"They'll not run again," he reassures Sister Mary Rose. "They'll not run and they'll not speak. This is a good lesson for them. We've been sent to teach right from wrong. You can only teach an animal through force. Leave them this way until I tell you otherwise. I am going to take a bath and wash their filth from me."

Sister Mary Rose pats my head. I feel myself glide into darkness.

5

I sit at my oak wooden desk, in my office lined with books. Books I brought from home. Books filled with the stories of Greeks and Romans. Books telling the stories of the people who came before me. Theological books that tell me of the real people. The first real people.

I sigh and try to remember what brought me to this place. I was always an eager student and wanted to only do well by my family. I want to succeed in my calling. My calling to the church and all the holiness within it. Instead, I am here in the rough western flat land. This place with dirty, dark Natives. This was an insult not only to my person but to my true calling to lead. I know that I am a natural leader, a natural speaker of God's word, but to place me in these rough wooden walls in this godforsaken place...this is offensive to my intellect and abilities.

Today my superior, Bishop LaFlamme, is visiting. It is part of the Bishop's duties to check up on the residential schools outside of Winnipeg. I straighten my back and fold my hands in prayer. I ask God for his direction and guidance during this day. This full day with the Bishop here to observe the school and the children. I thumb the pages of the written report on the successes of the school and my eyes fall on a short excerpt:

The children are learning the proper way to speak, to read and to write. The children have every moment of their day occupied. They are up at six in the morning and breakfast is over by seven. They attend mass from seven to eight and are in their desks by a quarter past eight. Classes are until half past eleven and lunch extends to half past twelve. Thirty minutes of playtime in the small fenced yard is allowed and the children are in class again by one o'clock. School ends at half past three and each student is assigned various chores. The boys help in the chopping and stacking of wood. The girls are in the kitchen washing dishes and helping the cook.

Every day the children are taught about the importance of cleanliness. Yes, cleanliness is as close to Godliness as they can become. I have taught them the rigours of hand washing and hair washing and will ensure the Bishop that each child is bathed once a week. That's one more time a week than any of them ever received at home.

I pace around my desk, worried about the arrival of my Bishop. These children have received more understanding of life since they have been under my care than their parents could ever provide. They have learned what it is like to sleep on a bed. They have learned to repeat their prayers from memory. They have learned the importance of fearing God. Ah, yes, the list I will report to my Bishop. I imagine the praise I will receive and if I continue to work so very hard, perhaps, just perhaps they will move me out of this school and onto the higher things I am destined for.

6

A small knock at the door brings me back to reality.

Sister Mary Rose enters with her head bowed and says, "Bishop LaFlamme's carriage is arriving. We are preparing the children to stand along the entrance steps."

"Very good! Very good! Let us go, Sister, and greet our most Holy Superior!"

Strutting down the hallway I realize that I am excited. I quiver with the anticipation of being able to kneel before my Bishop and kiss his Holy ring. My body is charged and I feel stirrings beneath my black robe. I am completely lost in this moment. This is my moment to be noticed. This is my time. I have toiled and laboured at this school for one full year. I want my report to glow in the presence of my superior. I am filled with the glory of this moment, but don't want anyone to notice my carnal enthusiasm.

Bishop LaFlamme steps down from the creaking carriage and I fall to one knee. I cross myself and whisper, "Your Excellency. Bienvenue à notre humble école." I reach for the Bishop's ringed hand and kiss the ring over and over again. I am lost in this great trilogy of man and his superior and God. I cannot stop kissing this ring until the Bishop wrestles his hand out of my grasp.

"Arrête!" whispers Bishop LaFlamme. "Cesse de faire ça immédiatement." His eyes question mine.

"Pardonnez-moi, Votre Grâce," I mutter rising to my feet.

"Children!" I call out as I straighten my black robe and put my large cross back into place. "Children! Say hello to His Excellency, Bishop LaFlamme!"

I nod to Sister Mary Rose, signalling her to slap the oldest children's lower backs. She leads the group in a merry, "Salut!

Bonjour, Votre Excellence!" and all the children start to sing, "Full in the Panting Heart of Rome."

It sounds absolutely terrible. The voices of the children reel and lurch over the opening words and as they reach the first refrain of, "God bless our Pope, God bless our Pope, God bless our Pope, the Great, the Good."

I race ahead and demand that the singing stop, raising both of my hands before this approaching train wreck. Out of the crowd steps Margarite and starts to do jumping jacks. Suzanne steps up beside her; then Therese joins her sisters. They slap their hands and feet together. The rest of the children join in. I have become the Ringmaster to these unstoppable savages. I taste the coals of hell dancing on my tongue.

My planned respectful greeting of Bishop LaFlamme has become a circus. There are snorts and chuckles and soon the boys in their woollen grey pants are rolling on the ground. Somersaults on one side and jumping jacks on the other.

"You see this, Bishop? This is what I must tolerate every day!" I yell as I reach for Margarite. She slides from my grasp and runs towards the Bishop. I lunge after her. Margarite reaches for the Bishop's gold robe at the same moment I raise my hand as far as my reach allows. I aim my fist. My arm descends towards the insufferable little black target when I feel the Bishop's hand wrap itself around my wrist. I freeze, become a statue with one raised fist. Silence fills the school yard.

Calmly, ever so calmly, the Bishop glares at me and whispers, "Stop!" Bishop LaFlamme slides the palm of his hand about Margarite's face and turns her eyes towards his. He gasps at the bruises and moans when he sees her swollen tongue dangling from her mouth.

Time slows. Bishop LaFlamme sinks to his knees, cupping his hands on either side of Margarite's cheeks. Between his tears, he mutters "Veuillez lui pardonner" and kisses each of her eyes. His compassionate face hardens as he looks at me and nods towards the school.

7

I am sweating. My heart won't stop racing and I fidget with the large rosary dangling from my neck. What am I to do, to say? Those damn little girls, all three of them. Nothing but trouble. Nothing but problems. My tribulation is them. I will explain that to him. He will understand. I sit myself behind my desk and clasp my hands together to form one large shaking fist. I feel my knees quivering and I can't stop the nervous earthquake erupting from my body.

There is tapping at the door and Sister Mary Rose swings it open. Bishop LaFlamme enters the room, his back hunched. He walks with the careful steps of the elderly. I bolt from my chair, but he stops me before I've even risen. Sister Mary Rose gasps and turns sharply to leave the room. Bishop LaFlamme turns his head towards her and says firmly, "Stay!"

The Bishop makes his way behind my desk. Clearing his throat, he looks at Sister Mary Rose and me. We are like two black chess pawns dressed in our Catholic uniforms. A pair of black and white people, our faces blanched, our eyes trembling in fear.

Bishop LaFlamme clears his throat, "Explain yourself!"

I swallow hard. My Adam's apple bobs.

"Your Excellency, this is not an easy post. I've worked hard, as has Sister Mary Rose to..." The Bishop raises his hand, signalling me to stop.

"You," he points to Sister Mary Rose. "You tell me what is happening in this place. How does a tiny little girl, a child of God like all other children in this world end up with blackened eyes and a tongue hanging from her lips?"

"Discipline is required, Your Excellency," whispers Sister Mary Rose. "Discipline and order. Some of the children, they just don't seem to want to accept these things." She lowers her eyes as she speaks.

"Discipline! The Lord talks about discipline, yes. He also speaks amply of love and compassion and of controlling your temper. Think of Proverbs 14:29."

He turns to me. "You are a blight on our faith—shame! Shame on you!" Bishop LaFlamme stands by the window, surrounded by sunlight. "I will be taking that child back with me to the city. My staff will come and inspect this place weekly and various priests will come and inspect each child for bruising. If one child has but one small, singular bruise anywhere—and I mean anywhere—on their bodies, you will both be dismissed from the Catholic faith permanently!"

I draw a deep breath. "But your Excellency, you don't understand how unruly they are. They are like animals. They don't obey. They don't do anything they are supposed to and little Margarite, the child you saw today—well she, she, she is a heathen creature!"

"You have taken Holy vows! Do you remember them?" asks the Bishop. "A vow, a solemn promise before and to God: Chastity, Poverty, and...yes, Obedience."

He turns back to Sister Mary Rose. "Get me that little girl. Bring her to me now!"

Sister Mary Rose scurries from the room to fetch the little brat. I feel rebellion pouring into my veins. "Your Excellency, don't take her. She has two sisters here. Shouldn't we try to keep these children together?"

"Why?" mutters Bishop LaFlamme, "So you can continue to beat her? No!"

Bishop LaFlamme leans into me. I can feel the heat of his breath. "Not one bruise—understood?"

8

Margarite sits beside the Bishop on his way back to Winnipeg, her head bobbing up and down in rhythm with the clacking horse hooves. Bishop LaFlamme looks over to her and smiles. Margarite sends a crooked smile back to his dancing eyes.

"My little one, ma petite," whispers the Bishop, "I will ensure your life will be without harm." Bishop LaFlamme pats Margarite's tiny hand.

"As our Great Lord is my witness, your life I will improve." Bishop LaFlamme shakes his head once more. His thoughts travel back to when the Canadian government offered his Church the money to run these schools. The government had presented this schooling of little aboriginal children as a great opportunity.

"Ah, Mon Dieu," thinks Bishop LaFlamme. "It could have been something of beauty. But look at what we have done. Look at this little one next to me. Forgive us."

Bishop LaFlamme squeezes Margarite's hand.

"This child, I swear to you Lord, will make a difference."

Bishop LaFlamme dreams of the life that he can give her. It will not be a fairy-tale life, but it will be a life that will not have fear and harm. He swears to himself, he will give to this child a life of security and understanding.

"I am an old, old man," he says turning to Margarite, "but you my little one, ma petite, you will make me young again and give me a reason for living. I will give you a life that will make our Lord proud." He places Margarite's tiny hand into his and lifts her tiny palm to his mouth where he plants a tiny kiss of hope.

9

"'Not one bruise...' That idiot! He doesn't know...How can he? He sits in Sacre Coeur day in and day out and has not one concept of what I have to deal with here. Not one bruise! I'll make sure of that!" I slam my body into my chair, fatigued from the emotional stress of the last two hours.

"Sister Mary Rose!" I shout, "Venez ici! Maintenant!"

The heavy door scrapes open. "Oui?" whispers Sister Mary Rose.

I motion my long fingers towards the chair opposite me. "S'asseoir!"

Sister Mary Rose moves into the chair. It is as if by moving as gradually as possible, she hopes my residual anger will evaporate.

"Do you know who I am, Sister?"

Sister Mary Rose only stares directly at me.

"I am the number one graduate of Loyola. Number one! My father, he knew that the English would take over the world and he sent me to that school. I learned to read, write and speak English perfectly. Not one trace of an accent. And after that, do you know what I did? I became the number one graduate of Saint-Sulpice—number one! And this is where I am—some isolated back woods dumping ground in Northern Manitoba. Northern Manitoba! Dear God, no one on earth ever comes here by choice. Never by choice! Do you understand what I am saying, Sister?"

I sense the uncontrolled rage in my eyes. "I am more than this! I am better than this…this wasteland! This pigsty of little Indians and Eskimos and cross-breed Métis. I was destined for bigger things, better things!"

Sister Mary Rose slowly raises her head. I see her fear. "Oui, Père LePage?"

I regain my composure. "He said 'no bruises' and we will comply. How much wood is there for heating this maison de fous, this nuthouse?"

"I can check. I don't know."

"Well, I have an idea. Those little girls. Those sisters of Margarite. It's time that they paid for the sins of their sister. They can chop all the wood that we need here! It can be their personal act of contrition!"

"But, Father LePage, they are but young girls. It would not be fair…"

"Fair! Get them in here. Let me tell them of their new duty."

Sister Mary Rose stands and slowly repeats the words of the Bishop, "Lui pardonner, Dieu."

10

"That man in the gold dress took her. Now what happens to us?" I ask. "Puhuliak, now what happens?"

"That's not my name. You know it's Suzanne. That's what you call me here—got it? And you, you are Therese. In this place that is who we are. We do what they tell us. We don't make a sound and then we are not taken away by an old man in a gold dress. We are together. We help each other. It's the way our mothers taught us. No isuigusuttuq. Understood?"

Me, Therese, I was always in the middle of everything. The one who had to do whatever either sister wanted, the middle girl.

"Of course, angajuk—I mean Suzanne. Of course. How long do we have to sit in these chairs? Where is Father LePage? Hikwa called him 'siquttipaa'," I giggle.

"Don't you even whisper that! Don't speak our language when we are here. You know what happens if they catch us," says Suzanne as she reaches into her own mouth and pulls on her own tongue and crosses her eyes.

I can't help but burst into laughter. Suzanne chuckles and reaches for my hand.

"We are here. We are together. Nothing will break us apart. One day we'll get out of here and we'll find our Hikwa and we will all go home." Suzanne tightens the grip on my hand. "But for now, we speak their tongues. This English and this French and we are good students. We will get out of here, Angavidiak—we will."

I turn my head towards her. Our eyes shine with the tears of trust. The same water in our eyes. We nod together.

Our moment is broken by the whoosh of the office door.

"Come!" demands Father LePage. "Quick!"

Suzanne and I stand like tin soldiers in front of him. We are as tall as we can make ourselves while our knees tremble like Arctic moss leaves on a cool, windy, spring day.

"Girls—I have a special work order for you. This is a big place and it needs much heat. Do either of you understand me?" asks Father LePage as he leans in so close that we each can smell his horrible breath. We see his blackened teeth and we each move back slightly.

"Don't shrink away from me! Oh little ones, you will do the most wonderful act of contrition. One that I believe has been sent to me from Sainte Louise de Marillac herself. Not that either of you little heathens would know her but still let us say this is almost a small miracle. Something you may understand."

Father LePage reaches behind his desk and lifts an axe in each of his hands.

"From now on my little darlings, you will help with the cutting of the wood for this place. You can attend school in the mornings only but will be out in the forest from noon until the supper hour. It will be good for you. It will make you even stronger than you already are. Here, my little ones. Here are your very own, personal crosses of redemption! Put out your hands!"

Father LePage walks towards us and our trembling hands reach up for our axes. Leaving the office I hear Suzanne whisper, ""Lui pardonner, Dieu."

11

Slap, chop. Slap, chop. Whoosh. Another tree slides to the ground. Bam. Bump. Beside me I can hear my sister's echoing hatchet. Slap, chop, slap, chop, whoooossshhh. Over and over again, me and Suzanne are ricocheting woodsmen.

In the past few weeks, a young white man named Joshua has driven us here in his Ford half-ton black truck. We help him lift the trees part way onto the truck bed and he hauls them a few yards down the road. Joshua will chop the chunks into blocks to be used in the fires of the residential school.

I had thought I would hate this but I don't. I don't mind the work no matter what the weather. It means I don't have to sit in that desk in the afternoon. We get to spend time outside. Outside, where we belong. Where we feel free. Sister Mary Rose sneaks us a snack some days. Extra bits of cheese and bread get tucked inside our cloth coats as we leave the school in Joshua's truck at noon.

Joshua is the only white boy I've ever talked to. He asks us all kinds of questions and when we answer he doesn't understand.

"How old are you two?"

"What's that mean?" I ask him.

"You know, how many years have you been alive? You look like you're around fourteen or so. I mean, you're skinny and that one next to you isn't. But you both look around the same age."

"Suzanne? What does he mean?" I ask looking at Suzanne who is falling asleep in the truck, her head bouncing against the passenger window. She is the elder sister, the anajuk. It is what I have been taught. The elder is to answer questions. I dig my sharp elbow into her ribs.

"AAIII—what's with you?" Suzanne screams as she starts to cough. "What are you doing to me?"

"He wants to know how old we are. What does that mean?" I am stuck in the middle of the truck seat. The shift stick knocking on the insides of each of my knees. The road is bumpy and I'm always the one in the centre of his questions.

"Oh, that—I am, in your years, going on fifteen. Therese is coming up to fourteen. We were each born when the first snows came. In your time it is called 'fall.' We don't mark our time in months and year numbers like you do. We count seasons. But not anymore." Suzanne knows she has said too much. Suzanne knows she isn't supposed to compare us with the whites. At least, not out loud.

I whisper to her, "Suzanne, remember we are good students. We will learn to talk in their French and their English and we will stay out of trouble. Just laugh now. He won't get it anyway. Just laugh." Joshua joins us.

"Ha—seasons. That's funny. How long you been at the school?"

How old? How long? How many more questions is he going to ask? We were taught that we never ask a stranger questions—ever! We were taught that they speak and we listen. We don't ever once ask anything even if we want to. We know that the right words will come and we will get our answers in a different way. There are many ways to find the answers. Watching is best.

The stick shift is bouncing between my thighs and I push my back hard against the seat. She has to say the words. Not me.

"We both came to the school when we were around nine years old." Suzanne has picked a number.

"That's a motherfuckin' long time to have put into that hell hole," says Joshua as he lights a home-rolled cigarette. For some reason the smell doesn't bother me here. Not like when Dad came home full of this stench. In Joshua's truck the smell makes sense.

"And you've been cuttin' trees for the last—how long?"

"About four winter seasons now," sighs Suzanne. "About that."

"Shit, you girls are tougher than most of the guys I know. Hey, you want a smoke?" Joshua hands his tobacco pouch to me. I hand it over to Suzanne. She hands it back to me, saying, "No thanks." I take a cigarette out of the pouch and squeeze it softly. Suzanne shakes her head, but I keep playing with it.

"Ah, take it," says Joshua, his own cigarette splashing ashes all over the truck cab. "You never know when you might want to have a puff. Here, take some matches too." I put the cigarette and matches inside the only bra I own. Joshua bursts out laughing. Suzanne and I join in. This is the most fun we've had with Joshua since he's been driving us.

When we started to cut wood we only cut in the area around the school. Father LePage found out that a local mill was hiring area farmers and paying them to cut. He signed us up saying that this would be our financial act of contrition. At last we could add to the much needed money for the running of the school.

He was smart about things though. Father LePage always made sure that we were in our desks on inspection day. The third Monday of every month. On Sundays we attended High Mass. It was our only afternoons that were spent away from the woods. Father LePage is the meanest white man I had ever known. I had hoped that I would never know another white guy until Joshua came into our lives.

Joshua tells us he is eighteen. He was raised on a farm and only went to school to Grade Four. He tells us about his mean, "bastard dad" who thought the purpose of having children was to have them work the farm. He tells us stories about his dad chasing him to beat him for not working hard enough. Joshua ran away when he was fourteen and came closer to the city. He couldn't find any work there and found some on another farm. A lumber mill opened not far from Winnipeg and Joshua went to work there. He cuts trees in the morning by himself and picks us up each working day at noon. This is what I mean—you don't have to ask white people questions. They will tell you everything whether or not you want to hear it.

Joshua is nice to us. He lets us take breaks with him and he talks about his nights of drinking with his friends in the small town of Pine Falls. He talks about Indian women and how they look just like us. Suzanne and I never say a word. We don't tell him that we don't like Indians. Our mothers taught us to never like them. Said they were double-faced, saying one thing in front of you and the opposite as they walk away.

Today is the first day I have kept something that belonged to a white man. A cigarette. I can smell the sour tobacco tucked away in my shirt. I feel the tingle of having done something terrible. I giggle to myself. I'm proud of this one small act of revenge against Father LePage and all he represents. I am being naughty and I love it. Joshua stops the truck and Suzanne and I lift our axes. We are ready for another afternoon in the cold fall air.

"Hey, hey now," says Joshua. "What about that smoke—shouldn't you light that up before you go to work today?"

"Not right now," I say with a smile. "Let's get our work done first."

"OK. But we're gonna have a smoke together before this day is over. Alright?"

I like Joshua. He has the kindest brown eyes that I have seen since I last saw my father's. He reminds me of home.

12

Every day in the bush I think of Hikwa. I do this because I am afraid that I will forget her. I am afraid that I will forget her perfect eyes. The sound of her voice. The tinkle in her laugh. Her energy. I wish for the day that I see her again. In my mind I will give her the best life imaginable. A life happier than mine is.

We hear she is the best student at her school. The best athlete with the highest average in French in the province in Manitoba. She is famous that way. Her bedroom must be a place filled with ribbons and trophies. The gold dress smiles each time she shows him a new one. He ruffles her hair and always says, "Tu es mon champion."

If I could see the way Hikwa can, I would see that her life is not perfect. She is an Eskimo in a white school. I would see how the other girls laugh at her shortness, at her straight black, bristly hair and all her "Inukshuk." I would see how she ignores those girls because at night Papa LaFlamme's eyes beam at her.

But I have only my imagination, not sight, and in my imagination they always have dinner together in a candle lit room. A room of quiet. A room of peace. A room of safety.

"My little one," he says, "Say the Hail Mary for me. First in English, then in French and tonight, lastly, in Spanish."

In my dreams of her, Hikwa knows many languages. She is smart and kind to the gold dress.

Clearing her throat first, she opens with, "Hail Mary full of grace. Je vous salue, Marie, pleine de grâce Dios te salve Maria, llena eres de gracia..."

I grin at the thought of her talking in all sorts of ways. Hikwa is clever and strong. I often wonder if a dull loneliness aches inside of her like it does in me. But I know that whatever is inside of each of us, our ways will never leave us. We were taught to always know what is ahead, behind and beside us as we walk about our days. To study the earth. We were taught to know the wind, the moon, and the stars. We are Inuk. They can't take that from us.

I wonder if she remembers me. I wonder if she remembers the faces of our mothers. My biggest fear is to have all of their faces wilt from each of our memories.

13

"Hey, do you girls want to come out to a dance at the Legion?" We are taking our break with Joshua. Fifteen minutes each afternoon.

Joshua, he always says words we don't understand. He has built us a beautiful fire and we are boiling a pot of water to make tea. Heavy, wet snowflakes fall from the grey sky. I am darting my head back and forth trying to catch snowflakes on my tongue before they melt over the fire. A game I used to play at home. Suzanne is sitting on the stump next to mine, rubbing her hands together and stamping her feet. We look at each other and shrug.

"A dance. Do you want to come out to a dance?"

Suzanne shakes her head but I know she doesn't understand it any more than I do.

"Do you girls even know what a dance is?" asks Joshua, pulling a cigarette out of his heavy jacket and handing one to me.

"No," I say as I spin the cigarette between my fingers. I snap it up into the air and lean in and catch it between my lips. Suzanne laughs. I pull the match from my bra and strike it against a rock, lighting the small tube in one flashy motion. Suzanne laughs even harder.

"You girls are dumb. You know it? I asked you if you wanted to go to a dance. Friday night. OK?"

"What's a 'dance'?" I ask with a glint in my eye. This should be fun. "Show us."

Joshua moves towards Suzanne and wraps one arm around her bulging waist. Takes her tiny, chubby fingers from one hand and holds them high into the air. He hums a song. I watch Suzanne shuffle out of step. Plunking her square feet onto his and each time, Joshua winces and wrestles his boots out from under hers. He starts to sing, "My Sister and I." At first we all laugh at his attempt, but as the song progresses our laughing turns to silence. Joshua doesn't understand.

Joshua croons words that talk about fear and the sky. His song ends with night time and crying.

Suzanne pulls her hand from his and plops back down on her stump. I sit on the ground next to her and hold the hand that was just in Joshua's. I toss my smoke into the flames. We both stare into the fire. Tears are sliding down Suzanne's face.

"What? What now? Shit, you girls. Here, I'll get the water." Joshua pours the hot water and we each take a turn dipping our shared tea bag into our tin mugs.

"I don't get it. What did I do wrong?" asks Joshua. "OK, and whatever it was that I done wrong, I'm truly sorry for it. Alright? I don't get you girls at all." Joshua shakes his head and pulls another butt from the deck.

Suzanne and I squeeze our hands together. I know that it is not my place to speak. I wait for Suzanne to say the words that will help Joshua understand.

"It's the song, Joshua. Not you," Suzanne whispers, rubbing her thick palms across her high cheek bones. I copy what she is doing. The tears and the thick snowflakes have turned my face to mud.

"I never heard those words before you said them. I never knew that people wrote songs like that for everyone to hear. We only hear hymns at school." Suzanne says. She is avoiding the real story. I play along. This is how it is supposed to be with the white people. Only tell part of the truth. Never the whole truth.

"Wow, a song by Jimmy Dorsey can make you bawl like a calf stuck in barbed wire! Holy Shit! If Jimmy only knew the effect he had on women...man that guy must get laid a lot." Joshua blows onto his mug and sits down on the ground next to Suzanne.

"Geez, you two...I'm sorry. I really am."

I hop up onto my feet and take Suzanne's hands into my own. "Come, sister—we will show him the music from home!"

I look over at Joshua and say, "Watch this. Jimmy Dorsey, my ass!"

I lean in close to Suzanne's mouth and with my lips smiling, taking a big breath I say, "Ooooma OOooma OOOoma!"

Suzanne replies, "A-Yuk A-Yuk A-Yuk." High pitched like the birds coming to shore for a landing.

I place my hands on her forearms, she puts her tiny palms on my forearms and together we mix our sounds. The sounds we know best. The sounds we were born to sing.

"Ooma A-Yuk A-Yuk Omma A-Yuk." It all becomes one giant sound with only the earth understanding what we are saying. We sway back and forth and change the pitch. We alternate between one being high and the other low tones. We are lost in the magic of what we know best. The sounds we first heard in our mothers' wombs. We sing for a long time and end our song with a long, swaying hug.

"Hey! That's ritzy. Can I try?"

I step back and Joshua wraps his large hands around Suzanne' forearms.

He takes a big breath and out of his mouth falls something that sounds like a sneeze. We all burst out laughing. He takes another big breath and a giant burp fills the air, the kind that sounds as if your vocal chords have snapped. We are laughing so hard that I bend over and let loose one of the longest, noisiest farts I've ever had.

Soon none of us can stand up. We are rolling on the ground like baby polar bears. Suzanne is turning into a very fat white woman with snow wrapping around her clothes in thick layers. I know that I have done one thing right today. I have made us both forget our real pain.

14

Father LePage is reviewing the ledgers.

"Something is not right here..." he says aloud as he twists a strand of hair with his left index finger. It is a habit of confused thought that has lasted from his childhood.

He takes the ledgers over to the small window because the snowflakes and frost are dimming the light in the room.

"The girls work for twenty cents a day...I am discounted fifty per cent of what I had to pay on the wood for this school because of their labour. This means I get $1.20 per week each on the girls, plus fifteen cents on each cord produced and I am only paying $1.00 per cord. Now take that wage over one month and.... It does not make any sense. These girls must not be working as hard as they used to. Their production appears to have dropped." He paces his office with the ledger in his right hand, twisting the hair on the left side of his head faster and faster as the confusion clears.

"The reality is, with the amount of cords they produce, I am making less on these girls than I did last fall!" He pauses. "Sister Mary Rose!" he shouts at the closed door.

Sister Mary Rose feels her head bolt up from her desk outside Father LePage's office. She feels the same sharp pain jolt through her stomach. The pain that snaps like lightning inside of her every time he shouts her name. She hates these moments. These moments where she is made to bear the brunt of his wrath. Sister Mary Rose politely taps on the wooden door and enters looking at the floor.

"Yes, Father?"

"Look me in the eyes. For the love of God, Sister Mary Rose, look me in the eyes. I am tired of looking at the top of your tunic!"

Sister Mary Rose raises her eyes. They are filled with fear, but today there is something else, too. A remnant from Bishop LaFlamme's words.

"What is going on with Suzanne and Therese?"

"They are good girls, Father. They do such good school work each morning and they keep our fires burning here in the afternoons. I don't understand why you are asking."

"I have been reviewing the ledgers and I have discovered a discrepancy!" This is what she fears most—his "discrepancies." One after another. "Discrepancies" in the kitchen. In the number of candles used during mass. In the little boys who he thinks are sipping the communal wine. Father LePage smells out discrepancies like a dog.

"Look at these ledgers, Sister. You see, it is in black ink on white paper. See!"

Sister Mary Rose leans in towards the desk and examines the jumble of numbers running in crooked columns off the page in front of her.

"See! You cannot tell me otherwise! Those little bitches— ah Mon Dieu, forgive my English. Those little girls. They are not PRODUCING!" he snarls. Grabbing the ledger from beneath Sister Mary Rose's nose, he shouts, "I have PROOF! I am getting to the very bottom of this. I will take this to the Bishop. That man and his 'No Bruises.' I'll show him!"

Sister Mary Rose feels the bile rising to the top of her throat, the acid stinging in her windpipes. Clasping her mouth with her right palm she flees from the room and retches into the trash container beside her own small desk. She wipes the sweat from her forehead and looks up in time to see Father LePage gush past her.

He stops at the door and turns back to Sister Mary Rose. "You say they are out in the woods with a boy, yes?"

Sister Mary Rose nods. Her hands have anchored themselves tight to the corner of her desk.

"Father LePage," Sister Mary Rose says, clearing her throat and feeling her heart race against her chest. "Father, it is a poor day to be heading off to the woods!" For the first time she can remember, she speaks clearly and with authority. "Why not go tomorrow? Or whenever this weather clears?"

Father LePage stares at her. He appears confused by her outburst.

"Why Sister, you have never...I mean, I have never heard you speak so much. What you say makes sense. It is poor weather and the girls should be back within the hour." He glances at the huge grandfather clock stationed by the school entrance.

"Perhaps I am acting in haste. Yes, I think you are correct. I will go another day. A day without snow and perhaps some sunshine. Yes." He puts his coat back onto the rung, straightens the cap on his head, closes the door of his office behind him.

15

Bishop LaFlamme clears his throat and looks into Margarite's eyes. Their pupils bulleted upon one another. One in anger, and one with the softness that was always there.

"Please, sit, assi ma chérie." Bishop LaFlamme says with a small laugh. He has adapted a rhyme that brings back a memory of his own mother.

Margarite sits tall in the high-back chair. Like a wolverine ready to pounce on her subject. Every muscle in her body is ready to recoil. She is on guard, aware of everything around her. Her intuition is on the hunt.

"When I was a young boy in France, so many decades ago, my own Mama would tell me, 'Assi mon osti' and we would laugh at her little poem—her attempt at humour. It became a small joke between us and as I got older I would say this to her when we would go out in the evenings for our meal. I am an old man but I still miss her. She died decades ago but somehow I can still feel her, in here," Bishop LaFlamme points to his heart.

Margarite does not blink. She looks at him and sneers, "At least you grew up with your own mother. I do not have that same privilege."

"Yes, I realize this." Bishop LaFlamme clears his throat, continuing to look directly at her. He does not blink or move his eyes from her.

"My purpose this morning in having you come to this office before you head off to school is twofold. Firstly, please tell me the scripture from Ephesians 4:26."

Margarite does not hesitate. She is first in all her classes. "Be ye angry, and sin not: let not the sun go down upon your wrath."

"Now," Bishop LaFlamme is interrupted by a moist, mucus-filled cough. He pulls a cotton hankie from his side pocket and fills it with green and yellow goo. Streaks of red snake through his handkerchief. Margarite's eyebrows rise ever so slightly.

"Pardon me. It seems as I age my lungs like to remind me that I will not be here forever." Bishop LaFlamme rolls the square cloth into a spongy ball and squeezes it back into his hidden pocket.

"I have come to a decision. Something I wrestled with last night. As you have said, and you are correct, I was very privileged to be raised by my own dear mother. I cannot give you your mother but I can do this one thing—I can take you to see your sisters."

Margarite's pulse picks up but she does not smile. She does not change her stoic stance. She remains erect in her chair. She feels her jaw tighten. She cannot release any sign of joy.

"They remain at the school with Father LePage and as far as I know, no injury or physical harm has ever occurred to them. I have had my people watching over that school to enforce a rule I presented to him the day I took you from there. No child is ever to exhibit a bruise. He has, as far as I know, maintained that regulation."

Margarite does not flinch. Her hands remain gripped to the arms of the chair. Her mouth is a straight line. Emotionless.

"I make an annual trip to the school. Usually in late spring, but because I think it is important for you to see your sisters, we will go this coming Saturday. Five days from now. We will take the sledge."

An uncomfortable silence strolls into the room and stands before Margarite and Bishop LaFlamme. Margarite's mind is spinning. He has gone to see them four times before this. She feels anger crawling up their wall of silence. Saint Paul—"Be ye angry, and sin not." She repeats the words over and over again silently.

"Does this please you?"

"Yes, Papa LaFlamme. Very much. I look forward to our trip together—and Papa, I thank you for this opportunity. I have longed to see them again." She stands before Bishop LaFlamme and takes his right hand. Leaning in towards his ring, she places a quiet kiss upon it.

"Very well. Head off to school then and I will see you at dinner tonight."

Bishop LaFlamme sits at his desk and wonders why he did not see a reaction of excitement from his young ward. He expected more. She has become very controlled, he thinks. She has lost her spontaneity. He puts it down to her age as he pushes back his heavy chair and pulls himself upward. The effort makes his cough return and he stands by his desk heaving and hacking.

Margarite hears the echo of his cough as she walks away from Bishop LaFlamme's office. She thinks perhaps she should have offered the old man a hug or at least a hand-shake, but she does not want to touch him. She has seen the blood balled up in his handkerchief. He does not have long left. That means she does not have long left in this place. Like the wolverine, Margarite forms a plan in her mind. She must. She knows that once her Papa LaFlamme is gone she will be returned to the horror of Father LePage.

16

Saturday, our one full day in the woods. No half day at school like the other five mornings. Sometimes it feels like the longest day in the calendar but at least we are not scrubbing toilets. Joshua's song has become our song. It has become our anthem. The song we sing as we chop the trees to the ground. Sometimes we change the words, trying to make each other laugh.

"My sister and I remember still," I bellow in my best bari-tone voice.

"A tulip garden at an old Dutch mill," responds Suzanne in a high, squeaky soprano.

"Or, should that be..." I sing low and slow, "A penis in a windowsill." Dragging out the word "penis," I sing once more, "a peeeennnniiiisssss in a windowsill." We laugh again and continue our work on the tree. Sister and I no longer work separately. In the winter cold we have joined forces cutting each tree down together. Some days we work without speaking or singing but today Suzanne is in a good mood. We are singing together.

"And a home that was all our own until," Suzanne continues the song.

"We were picked up and shipped to hhhhelllll" I sing as loudly and in as manly a voice as I can manage. We continue our laughter and chopping.

I stop mid-swing. "Hey, I hear Joshua's truck. Is it time for break already?" I know Suzanne. She will take a break at any time of any day. She no longer uses the sun to know the time of day.

"Fine by me," says Suzanne, throwing her axe down into the snow. She never leaves it hanging from a tree the way I do. We have spent hours looking for her axe. I bend over and slice it into the bark beside mine. I don't want to have to look for it again today.

"I didn't even start a fire yet. Didn't even fill the pot with snow for tea. Maybe he isn't feeling well," I say to Suzanne as I reach inside my cloth coat for my half of a cigarette. I flick a match against a tree trunk. The tips of my fingers are red like the match tip in my fingerless gloves. Together we walk towards the clearing. I am puffing on my smoke. Suzanne continues to hum our song.

Getting closer to the truck we see there is someone inside the cab with Joshua. In slow motion the head turns towards the back window. The fierce face of Father LePage is frowning at both of us. We stop dead in our tracks. Snow is up to our knees and our long cold breath hangs in the air like blocks of ice between us and the truck.

"Run!" I scream. "Run, Angavidiak, aqpasuajuq!" Suzanne is standing in the same position as a statue of the Virgin Mother. I grab her hand tightly. Turning her around. Together we try to run as quickly as possible through the snow that is pulling onto our thighs, dropping us down into swirling swallows.

I can hear the shouts of Father LePage sounding closer to us. "Stop! You animals! Stop! You heathen bitches!"

His words are gaining ground but I continue to pull on Suzanne. We run back into the woods. Suzanne drops to her knees at the last tree that we were working on together. She heaves between deep breaths, "Stop. Iq. Puhuliak. We must stop." I know she cannot move any further. Our small attempt at escape is over.

"Les chiens!" screams Father LePage. His own breath coming in short gasps. Short gasps that seem to spur his rage.

"I knew you were up to no good. I knew it! Look at you smoking cigarettes and taking breaks early in the morning. Shame! Shame on you both!"

He lifts his arms into the air. Joining his fists, he drives them both onto the top of Suzanne's head with all his strength. Suzanne's body slumps onto the snow soundless as a hare. I reach over to the tree we were both working on, taking an axe into each hand.

"Fuck off, you fuckin' freak! I'm gonna chop you to pieces! You fucker!"

I swing my arms into the air and charge towards Father LePage, axes flailing and flying side to side. I have steel-tipped wings. In my rage I see nothing but the black wall of his robes. I know only that I am going to slice the wall open.

Joshua bolts between us. He snatches my wrists and twists them until I drop the axes.

"Get in the truck! Both of you! Get in the fuckin' truck!"

Joshua scoops Suzanne into his arms. I jump into the bed of the truck, laying Suzanne's head on my lap. I pull her touque off and place it under her head. I spit into the palm of each of my hands and rub circles of healing onto the bump at the top of Suzanne's head. I softly sing, "We are learning to forget the fear / That came from a troubled sky..." Suzanne's eyes flutter open.

17

The horse and sledge trudge through the whiteness that is winter. It is slow going for Bishop LaFlamme and he keeps a thick scarf around his mouth. The reins dangle between his knees. These horses have taken this route so often they do not need to be reminded of what direction to travel.

Margarite does not feel the cold the way he does. She feels the tingle of excitement as she sits perched on their bench, looking at the land. The forms. The shapes. The way the sun is making shadows fall onto the earth. The wind is north-north-east. They have travelled for about three hours. They have passed through two small villages. One has a small lumber mill. The other a large church. She has seen white people only. No Indians yet. They must be nearing their land, she thinks. She remembers the maps she studied at school. They must be nearing the place called Pine Falls.

She knows the trip will take five hours. She has studied the maps over and over again. She knows exactly what kind of land they are on. She knows where every creek and tiny lake exists. Every night for the past week she has hidden bread, cheese, and dry meat in the apron she wears at dinner time. She has also hidden her steak knife. Every morsel she has taken is in the pouch that lies hidden under the bench of the sledge. She is ready. She has to be.

Bishop LaFlamme is unable to speak very much. The cold air feels like tiny daggers piercing his lungs each time he takes a breath. He pushes his elbow into her side and points his head towards something he wants her to see. Something he thinks is of value.

Looking in the direction of where he is pointing, Margarite nods and says each time, "Yes, a big church. Not as big as ours though."

Her slanted eyes shine back at his. She is doing all she can to entertain him during their travels. She sings all the hymns that she knows by heart and repeats the "Hail Mary" in several different languages. Excluding her own.

They are nearing the last leg of their journey. She knows she has about one hour before she has to put her plan into action.

18

As we bump along in the back of truck, I can hear everything that they are saying in the cab. I look through the back window and watch them.

"You're a spineless little bastard aren't ya, Father? I was raised to respect the clergy. My dad used to say that men of the cloth were educated. That they did a job that no one else wanted to do. They carry the weight of all their parishioners on their shoulders. But you, you ain't nothin' but a spineless little bastard." Joshua leans over the steering wheel of the old truck and lights a cigarette.

"You're goin' to hell for what you did back there. To hell, Mister!"

Joshua continues to look straight ahead. His cigarette smoke fills the truck cab with a hazy fog. He glances back at Suzanne and me. We must look like a Christmas picture from school. The one with Mary and her baby cradled in her lap. Suzanne and I are the girls of his crèche.

"Your father was correct," I hear Father LePage sigh. "He's…how is it young people say now, 'Spot on!' I do carry the weight of the world on these shoulders. You have no idea what you're talking about. These heathens that I have to deal with at school each day. They are like dogs, they only under-stand physical punishment."

"Dogs? You're saying those girls back there are nothin' but dogs?"

"Exactly, that's why I call them bitches." Father LePage laughs. His robe jiggles. I can see the beads of his long cross rubbing together.

"You're one sick, sorry bastard!" Joshua shouts. He slams the brakes hard. Our bodies thud into the back window of the truck cab. He jumps out of the truck, "Sorry ladies," he whis-pers to us. He stomps his way to Father LePage's door and swings it open. In one quick move, he pulls Father LePage from the cab.

"Here's one from the girls!" he yells as his fist drives into the priest's nose.

"And here's one from me!" he roars as he plants his fist into Father LePage's ribs.

I laugh. The air in Father LePage's lungs splatters onto the heavy snow.

"Imaa!" I scream, clapping my hands high above my head. Suzanne wrestles herself into a sitting position but I gently place her head back into my lap.

Joshua lifts his boot into the air and stomps a solid crack onto Father LePage's left knee. "And that one is from all the other kids at the school!" Joshua picks up Father LePage's body and slams it back into the passenger side of the cab.

"And you'll never, I mean never, lay a hand on a girl again! You sick, sorry bastard."

The hot spit from Joshua's mouth sprays against Father LePage's beard and his eyes and what used to be his nose. He nods and slumps to the floor of the truck.

19

Bishop LaFlamme pulls the sledge up to the front of the school. There is no welcoming committee this time. He has not given advance warning of his visit.

Hikwa hops down from the sledge and raises both her hands to help him down. His body moves slowly and carefully, afraid to slip. Hikwa and Bishop LaFlamme walk up the snow-laden steps of the school living quarters. They pass by a brass bell dangling from the eavestrough of the roof. Hikwa snaps the rope suspended from its core. One quick, sudden bong punctures the cold air. The sound slides into the air for miles. Hikwa shivers from the memory this sound triggers. Sister Mary Rose heaves the heavy door open.

"Bishop! Dear God! Your Excellency! Come inside!" Sister Mary Rose's face is flushed with nervousness.

"No one told us you were coming, Your Grace!" Sister Mary Rose leans in to clutch onto one of Bishop LaFlamme's arms. "Here, let me help."

Bishop LaFlamme yanks his body up one step at a time, flanked on one side by Hikwa and Sister Mary Rose on the other. Hikwa steps back suddenly. Her head faces south. Her lips tighten. Her ears prickling from the sound of a vehicle in the distance.

"What's that?" she snaps.

"What?" Sister Mary Rose asks.

"That noise! What is it?" Hikwa loosens her grip on Bishop LaFlamme's arm.

Hikwa steps down and walks to the middle of the road. She stands ready to pounce behind the horse and sledge that brought her here.

Sister Mary Rose pushes against Bishop LaFlamme. He leans forward, almost squatting to grasp the step in front of him. She moves in front of him and takes his hands. "Come, Your Excellency," she coaxes. "Carefully."

"Margarite?" he asks as he looks into Sister Mary Rose's relieved eyes.

"Margarite!" yells Sister Mary Rose, "Bishop wants you. Please come."

Sister Mary Rose stares at the rigid profile of Hikwa. Her. She remembers her now. The other sister. You would never know she was one of them, Sister Mary Rose thinks. The sheen in her hair is almost blinding. Her fine city clothes. Mitts that keep her hands warm. She doesn't look like one of them at all. From a distance she could pass for a white woman, thinks Sister Mary Rose. Inside of herself she feels a small amount of jealousy.

The truck takes shape from the distance, and every muscle in Hikwa's body stands stiff. Ready to act. Ready for the contents of this machine. She knows what is in front of her, behind her and on either side. Winds at south-southeast. Sun to her left. Approximately 1 PM. Nearest town about seventeen miles away. Hikwa is ready. She doesn't move or cringe as the truck pulls to a stop six feet from her boots. She walks towards the driver door. Her eyes stare straight into Joshua's. There is no smile. There is no wave of a hand. There is only Hikwa ready to take down her prey.

Joshua rolls down his window and smoke from his cigarette escapes into the winter sky.

"Who the hell are you?" he asks in a gruff voice. Hikwa is not the only person who knows how to stand on guard.

"No, Mister, who the hell are you?" asks Hikwa, her hand sliding over the steak knife in her left pocket. Her fingers itch to have the blade within her grasp.

"Listen, lady, I'm just askin' a question. Bottom line, I'm just here to drop off some trash and then I'm turning this truck around and never coming back to this hell hole again." Joshua leans into the handle of the driver door and steps out from the truck. Turning his back to slap the door shut, he feels a sharp blade sticking hard into his ribs.

Joshua turns around. He looks into the eyes of someone he knows would kill. He raises both his arms. Angavidiak pops her head out from the truck bed.

"Hikwa?" She jumps from the truck bed. "Hikwa! Hikwa! Hikwa!" They are once again two little girls flying into each other's arms. The noise of their reunion crowds the winter air. They hold each other so tight neither one of them can breathe. Angavidiak steps back and motions for Hikwa to come.

"Angavidiak, takusaqpaa!"

Puhuliak cautiously raises her eyes only above the truck bed. "Ai-nukaq!" She flops one leg over the edge of the truck box. Sliding her second leg over the truck box, she loses balance and falls into the arms of her two sisters. They roll together on the winter ground. Laughing. Crying. Making the happy sounds of early springtime. The sisters become one giant snow angel.

"Hey, what's all this about?" asks Joshua. "That woman was ready to kill me and you girls are hugging her?"

"This is our sister, Hikwa. She was taken from us by that gold robe over there."

I point to the small veranda of the residence where Sister Mary Rose and Bishop LaFlamme stand. One mouth is hanging open wide, and the other is half-smiling.

"We thought we would never see her again. Never. Hikwa, this is our good friend Joshua. He's our driver for our wood-cutting job."

"Wood-cutting job?" Hikwa clutches a hand from each sister and pulls off their tattered gloves. She stares at their calloused hands.

"He makes you cut wood here?" Hikwa scowls. She lowers her voice, "You're not staying here. Go. Get your things both of you. I've brought stuff. This time we run. Far and fast. I have a plan. Go!"

"Listen," says Joshua, "I have a plan too."

He opens the passenger door. Out slithers Father LePage. His body lands on the earth with a dull thump. Sister Mary Rose screams and races towards him.

"My God, what is this? What have you done to him?"

Joshua doesn't answer. Instead, he turns to the three girls. "Get inside and pack whatever stuff you have. I'll wait out here to make sure nothing goes wrong."

Phuuliak and Angavidiak run inside.

Sister Mary Rose wraps her hands under Father LePage's armpits, dragging him towards the steps.

Hikwa walks up the stairs to Bishop LaFlamme. He smiles his kindly smile. "You go with my blessing, ma petite. My heart will die soon but it will die with the love you have filled it with in these last five years. I will say this to you only once. Je t'aime."

Margarite feels the tears rolling down her high cheek-bones. She wraps her arms around Bishop LaFlamme's sagging neck and whispers into his ear, "Je t'aime, Papa."

She kisses him lightly on the lips and steps back as Puhuliak and Angavidiak walk out onto the porch.

Joshua leans over and opens the passenger door of his truck, "Hop in, little ladies!"

The girls climb into the front seat and as they drive away, Hikwa turns and takes one last look. Bishop LaFlamme raises his old hand to his lips and blows her the kiss that will carry her home. Hikwa raises her hand and blows back the kiss that will carry him to heaven.

ACKNOWLEDGEMENTS

FOR MANY YEARS, I have written stories and put them away into a drawer. I would tell myself that I had "had a good write," smile and lock things away. One of the bravest things I have ever done, next to giving birth to and raising my sons, is to put a stack of stories into a large envelope. I kissed the envelope and whispered, "Have fun, girls." The envelope was addressed to Peter Midgley.

I thank you first Peter, for keeping my words safe and for seeing them in a way that I could not. Your protectiveness and deep care for these stories is what kept them out of the drawer. I thank Kimmy Beach for having copyedited this work with the expertise that only belongs to her.

To the University of Alberta Press, thank you for taking a chance with me.

GLOSSARY

aanauniq: *beauty*
aggaituq: *one who has no hands*
ajujuq: *run away*
amaq: *carry baby on back, in hood*
amauti: *woman's coat*
anaana: *mother*
anaanatsiaq: *grandmother*
angajuk: *older sibling*
angakkug: *shaman*
aniguititsijuq: *help through difficulty*
annituqtuq: *he survives destitution*
aqpasuajuq: *run*
aqqaqpuq: *eat rapidly*
arnaluk: *naughty woman*
anirniq: *spirit*
ataata: *daddy, father*
ataatatsiaq: *grandfather*

ataatavut qilangmitutit, atiit isumagitiartauli: *beginnings of the Lord's Prayer, "Our Father who art in heaven..."*

Atanarjuat: *the movie,* The Fast Runner *(2001), an Inuit legend*

attagu: *let's go!*

attigi: *caribou parka with fur inside*

aumajuq: *soft, unfrozen*

avasirngulik: *Elder*

Igjugarjuk: *name of shaman*

ii: *yes*

iima: *yes*

ijuqtajuq: *laughs easy*

ikauqpuq: *cross a river, long distance*

iksarikpuq: *done quickly, done well*

immaaluk: *old days*

imminuuqpug: *return home, to his own place, also goes into himself in thought*

inniavik: *the house one will visit after a long journey*

intu'dlit braids: *traditional Inuit women's braids, hair wrapped around hide*

inuttapuq: *get*

Inuttituuqpuq: *behave like an Inuk, speak like an Inuk*

inuuhuktuq: *boy*

isuaruti: *heal us, heal in physical or moral sense*

isuigusuttuq: *to be bad, evil*

isuinniluppuq: *things are bad*

isummaniq: *reached the age of reason*

isutsipaaq: *head dog, lead dog*

itsanitaq: *events that happened a long time ago*

kabloona: *white man*

kajuq: *red hair*

katitippat: *work at uniting things that were separated*

katjaarivaa: *misses it for a long time*

kiinarlutuq: *sad face, sore face, ugly face*

kinauvit: *who are you?*

krepik: *sleeping bag*

kuru: *In Japanese "to come"*

ma'na: *thank you*

mikigiatsapuq: *release traps*

mingippaa: *punches with his fist*

muktuk: *beluga or narwhal whale blubber used as food*

nakurami: *thank you for it*

nakuusiaq: *love received*

ninngappuq: *a child is in a rage*

padlei: *the HBC post from 1926 to 1960, the Caribou Inuit who lived*
close by in the Keewatin region of Northern Manitoba were also
called Padleimiut (or Padlirmiut, or Paallirmiut, or Patlirmiut)

pillurittitaq: *to treat as great*

pisiit: *songs of feelings, song with a drum only*

piujuq: *good*

piusiqtuqpug: *to pretend to be good*

pukaangajug: *snow that is good enough to make a snow house*

qalgiq: *ceremonial snowhouse*

qallunaaq: *white person, non-Inuit*

qallunaaqtaq: *Euro-Canadian cloth or clothing*

qallunaat: *Anglo-Canadian*

qatangutigiit: *a group, a group of siblings*

qugjuk: *Whistling Swan*

quik: *seal urine*

saimmavuq: *in peace*

saimu: *peace be with you*

saipaaqsauti: *something to make a sad person happier*

sanningajuliuqpaa: *make the sign of the cross over him, bless him*

sarimajuq: *happy to have what he has*

sarliaq: *carry on lap, shelter one's young*

siutaujaqtuqpuq: *Inuit string game*

siutiruq: *snail, spiral shell that looks like wrinkles*

takusaqpaa: *rise to see, seek to see, turn to see*

taliaq: *being on guard*

taliut: *caribou snot*

taima: *asking if it is ready, if it is time?*

tarniq: *breath soul*

tiguat: *hard part of whip*

tirlinaaqpaa: *plays him a trick quickly either in good or evil intent*

tunngahugit: *welcome*

tuktu: *caribou*

tungasuttuq: *feel at ease*

turaaqpuq: *precise aim*

turqavik: *where one feels at home, where one lives*

uarittuq: *person in soft snow*

ugguapuq: *misses him*

uhuk: *penis*

uisuppaa: *make love to him*

ukkuusimajuq: *of something caught in a trap*

ulu: *woman's knife*

unataqpaa: *to struggle against someone in a psychological sense*

ungavaa: *a kindly love, devoted to him*

upaluajaqpuq: *he immediately does what he says, he obeys well*

upaluajaqpuq: *obey well*

upirngasaq: *melting of snows, start of spring*

uppirijatsaq: *truth of faith*

uqarluatuq: *he talks fluently but bad humouredly*

usiqtuq: *lie down under blanket*

usuaqsimajuq: *trap that has its tongue broken*

uummatuq: *the soul comes back to the life of grace by the sacrament of penance*